The Problem of Cell 13

十三號死刑牢房

of Cell 13

商務印書館

Name of Book: The Problem of Cell 13
Author: Jacques Futrelle
Text adaptation and activities: Graeme and Silvia Thomson
Editors: Rebecca Raynes, Elvira Poggi Repetto
Design: Nadia Maestri
Illustrations: Gianni De Conno
Edition: ©1999 Black Cat Publishing
                  an imprint of Cideb Editrice, Genoa, Canterbury

系 列 名：Black Cat 優質英語階梯閱讀 · Level 6
書   名：十三號死刑牢房
責任編輯：黃淑嫻
封面設計：張　毅
出   版：商務印書館（香港）有限公司
          香港筲箕灣耀興道3號東滙廣場8樓
          http://www.commercialpress.com.hk
印   刷：中華商務彩色印刷有限公司
          香港新界大埔汀麗路36號中華商務印刷大廈
版   次：2004年2月第1版第1次印刷
          © 2004 商務印書館（香港）有限公司
          ISBN 962 07 1701 5
          Printed in Hong Kong

出版説明

　　本館一向倡導優質閱讀，近年來連續推出了以"Q"為標識的 "Quality English Learning 優質英語學習"系列，其中《讀名著學英語》叢書，更是香港書展入選好書，讀者反響令人鼓舞。推動社會閱讀風氣，推動英語經典閱讀，藉閱讀拓廣世界視野，提高英語水平，已經成為一種潮流。

　　然良好閱讀習慣的養成非一日之功，大多數初、中級程度的讀者，常視直接閱讀厚重的原著為畏途。如何給年輕的讀者提供切實的指引和幫助，如何既提供優質的學習素材，又提供名師的教學方法，是當下社會關注的重要問題。針對這種情況，本館特別延請香港名校名師，根據多年豐富的教學經驗，精選海外適合初、中級英語程度讀者的優質經典讀物，有系統地出版了這套叢書，名為《Black Cat 優質英語階梯閱讀》。

　　《Black Cat 優質英語階梯閱讀》體現了香港名校名師堅持經典學習的教學理念，以及多年行之有效的學習方法。既有經過改寫和縮寫的經典名著，又有富創意的現代作品；既有精心設計的聽、説、讀、寫綜合練習，又有豐富的歷史文化知識；既有彩色插圖、繪圖和照片，又有英美專業演員朗讀作品的 CD。適合口味不同的讀者享受閱讀之樂，欣賞經典之美。

　　《Black Cat 優質英語階梯閱讀》由淺入深，逐階提升，好像參與一個尋寶遊戲，入門並不難，但要真正尋得寶藏，需要投入，更需要堅持。只有置身其中的人，才能體味純正英語的魅力，領略得到真寶的快樂。當英語閱讀成為自己生活的一部分，英語水平的提高自然水到渠成。

商務印書館 (香港) 有限公司
編輯部

使用説明 _____

1 應該怎樣選書？

按閱讀興趣選書

《Black Cat 優質英語階梯閱讀》精選世界經典作品，也包括富於創意的現代作品；既有膾炙人口的小説、戲劇，又有非小説類的文化知識讀物，品種豐富，內容多樣，適合口味不同的讀者挑選自己感興趣的書，享受閱讀的樂趣。

按英語程度選書

《Black Cat 優質英語階梯閱讀》現設 Level 1 至 Level 6，由淺入深，涵蓋初、中級英語程度。讀物分級採用了國際上通用的劃分標準，主要以詞彙（vocabulary）和結構（structures）劃分。

Level 1 至 Level 3 出現的詞彙較淺顯，相對深的核心詞彙均配上中文解釋，節省讀者查找詞典的時間，以專心理解正文內容。在註釋的幫助下，讀者若能流暢地閱讀正文內容，就不用擔心這一本書程度過深。

Level 1 至 Level 3 出現的動詞時態形式和句子結構比較簡單。動詞時態形式以現在時（present simple）、現在時進行式（present continuous）、過去時（past simple）為主，句子結構大部分是簡單句（simple sentences）。此外，還包括比較級和最高級（comparative and superlative forms）、可數和不可數名詞（countable and uncountable nouns）以及冠詞（articles）等語法知識點。

Level 4 至 Level 6 出現的動詞時態形式，以現在完成時（present perfect）、現在完成時進行式（present perfect continuous）、過去完成時（past perfect continuous）為主，句子結構大部分是複合句（compound sentences）、條件從句（1st and 2nd conditional sentences）等。此外，還包括情態動詞（modal verbs）、被動形式（passive forms）、動名詞（gerunds）、

短語動詞（phrasal verbs）等語法知識點。

　　根據上述的語法範圍，讀者可按自己實際的英語水平，如詞彙量、語法知識、理解能力、閱讀能力等自主選擇，不再受制於學校年級劃分或學歷高低的約束，完全根據個人需要選擇合適的讀物。

② 怎樣提高閱讀效果？

　　閱讀的方法主要有兩種：一是泛讀，二是精讀。兩者各有功能，適當地結合使用，相輔相成，有事半功倍之效。

　　泛讀，指閱讀大量適合自己程度（可稍淺，但不能過深）、不同內容、風格、體裁的讀物，但求明白內容大意，不用花費太多時間鑽研細節，主要作用是多接觸英語，減輕對它的生疏感，鞏固以前所學過的英語，讓腦子在潛意識中吸收詞彙用法、語法結構等。

　　精讀，指小心認真地閱讀內容精彩、組織有條理、遣詞造句又正確的作品，着重點在於理解 "準確" 及 "深入"，欣賞其精彩獨到之處。精讀時，可充分利用書中精心設計的練習，學習掌握有用的英語詞彙和語法知識。精讀後，可再花十分鐘朗讀其中一小段有趣的文字，邊唸邊細心領會文字的結構和意思。

　　《Black Cat 優質英語階梯閱讀》中的作品均值得精讀，如時間有限，不妨嘗試每兩個星期泛讀一本，輔以每星期挑選書中一章精彩的文字精讀。要學好英語，持之以恆地泛讀和精讀英文是最有效的方法。

③ 本系列的練習與測試有何功能？

　　《Black Cat 優質英語階梯閱讀》特別注重練習的設計，為讀者考慮周到，切合實用需求，學習功能強。每章後均配有訓練聽、説、讀、寫四項技能的練習，分量、難度恰到好處。

聽力練習分兩類，一是重聽故事回答問題，二是聆聽主角對話、書信朗讀、或模擬記者訪問後寫出答案，旨在以生活化的練習形式逐步提高聽力。每本書均配有 CD 提供作品朗讀，朗讀者都是專業演員，英國作品由英國演員錄音，美國作品由美國演員錄音，務求增加聆聽的真實感和感染力。多聆聽英式和美式英語兩種發音，可讓讀者熟悉二者的差異，逐漸培養分辨英美發音的能力，提高聆聽理解的準確度。此外，模仿錄音朗讀故事或模仿主人翁在戲劇中的對白，都是訓練口語能力的好方法。

閱讀理解練習形式多樣化，有縱橫字謎、配對、填空、字句重組等等，注重訓練讀者的理解、推敲和聯想等多種閱讀技能。

寫作練習尤具新意，教讀者使用網式圖示（spidergrams）記錄重點，採用問答、書信、電報、記者採訪等多樣化形式，鼓勵讀者動手寫作。

書後更設有升級測試（Exit Test）及答案，供讀者檢查學習效果。充分利用書中的練習和測試，可全面提升聽、說、讀、寫四項技能。

❹ 本系列還能提供甚麼幫助？

《Black Cat 優質英語階梯閱讀》提倡豐富多元的現代閱讀，巧用書中提供的資訊，有助於提升英語理解力，擴闊視野。

每本書都設有專章介紹相關的歷史文化知識，經典名著更有作者生平、社會背景等資訊。書內富有表現力的彩色插圖、繪圖和照片，使閱讀充滿趣味，部分加上如何解讀古典名畫的指導，增長見識。有的書還提供一些與主題相關的網址，比如關於不同國家的節慶源流的網址，讓讀者多利用網上資源增進知識。

CONTENTS

Some Information about Jacques Futrelle's Life　　9
認識推理小説家傑克・福翠爾

The Story: *The Problem of Cell 13*　　10
《十三號死刑牢房》故事簡介

CHAPTER ONE

The Bet　　12
鬥智的賭局

ACTIVITIES　　22

Other Prison Stories　　26
以逃獄為題材的著名電影

CHAPTER TWO

Chisholm Prison　　30
銅牆鐵壁的死刑牢房

ACTIVITIES　　39

CHAPTER THREE

A Message from Cell 13　　44
由十三號牢房發出的神秘信息

ACTIVITIES　　51

Futrelle's Death on the *Titanic*　　55
葬身鐵達尼海難的傑克・福翠爾

CHAPTER FOUR

A Strange Voice 64

怪異的叫聲

ACTIVITIES 70

CHAPTER FIVE

Countdown to Freedom 76

恢復自由的最後倒數

ACTIVITIES 83

CHAPTER SIX

How Did He Do It? 86

他怎樣越獄成功？

ACTIVITIES 97

APPENDICES

Exit Test 101

升級測試

Key to the Activities and Exit Test 104

練習答案和測試答案

This story is recorded in full on the CD. 故事錄音

These symbols indicate the beginning and end of the extracts linked to the listening activities.

聽力練習開始和結束的標記

Some Information about Jacques Futrelle's Life

*J*acques Futrelle was born in Georgia in 1875 and died in 1912 at the age of 37, one of the unfortunate victims of the sinking of the *Titanic*. Futrelle was working as a journalist [1] on the editorial staff of the *Boston American* – now the *Boston Herald* – when the publication of *The Problem of Cell 13* in 1905 brought him fame. *Cell 13* was the first of a series of stories to feature [2] the scientific detective, Augustus S.F.X. Van Dusen, more commonly known as The Thinking Machine, a character who combines elements of Edgar Allan Poe's Auguste Dupin (note the similarity between the two first names) and Conan Doyle's Sherlock Holmes. Like Dupin and Holmes, Van Dusen was an example of the gentleman amateur [3] detective, men of independent means for whom solving crimes was more a hobby than a profession.

---

1. **journalist** : a person who writes news stories.
2. **feature** : give an important part to.
3. **amateur** : taking part in an activity just for pleasure, not as their job.

The Problem of Cell 13, like the other Thinking Machine stories, was first published in the newspaper where Futrelle worked, challenging the reader to find the solution.

When Futrelle went down with the *Titanic*, the world lost a fine journalist and a great master of the short story.

The Story: The Problem of Cell 13

The Thinking Machine, a remarkable, though somewhat eccentric [1] scientist who spends all his time in the lab inventing brilliant and outrageous [2] theories, decides one day to have a bet with two friends. He bets that a prisoner can escape from a cell using just his mind, and to prove it to his companions he decides to volunteer for the experiment himself. Locked in Cell 13 of Chisholm Prison and with no help from outside he must try to escape. But the prison is absolutely secure, its walls impossible to climb, the cell impossible to escape from and infested with rats.

Will he manage to win his bet? How?

---

1. **eccentric** : strange, unusual.
2. **outrageous** : shocking.

Before you read

1 **Fill in the text below using the adjectives in the box. Then listen to the CD and check if you were right.**

> strange   famous   thin   bizarre
>
> mental   little   small   blue   large
>
> profound   pale   unusual   thick
>
> yellow   brilliant

Professor Augustus S. F. X. Van Dusen's appearance was as
1................... as his name. He was 2................... with the thin
shoulders of a student and his face was extremely 3................... . His
eyes were the eyes of a man who studies 4................... things. They
were always half-closed in concentration. Although he wore
5................... glasses you could see that his eyes were 6................... .
But his strangest feature was his abnormally 7................... forehead,
on top of which sat a crown of 8................... hair. Together all these
things gave him a 9..................., almost grotesque personality.

Professor Van Dusen's family came from Germany. Many of his
ancestors had been 10................... scientists; he was the logical result,
the master mind. And logic was his passion. He believed that two
and two always equal four, except in 11................... cases, when they
may equal three or five. He believed that all things that start must go
somewhere and he was able to concentrate all the 12...................
force of his ancestors to solve any problem.

The public knew Van Dusen as The Thinking Machine and perhaps
this phrase described him best of all. He spent all his time in his
13................... laboratory where he invented 14................... theories
that shocked scientists and had a 15................... effect on the world.

CHAPTER ONE

The Bet

P rofessor Augustus S. F. X. Van Dusen's appearance was as strange as his name. He was thin with the thin shoulders of a student and his face was extremely pale. His eyes were the eyes of a man who studies little things. They were always half-closed in concentration. Although he wore thick glasses you could see that his eyes were blue. But his strangest feature [1] was his abnormally large forehead, on top of which sat a crown of yellow hair. Together all these things gave him a bizarre, [2] almost grotesque [3] personality.

Professor Van Dusen's family came from Germany. Many of his ancestors had been famous scientists; he was the logical result, the mastermind. [4] And logic was his passion. He believed that two

---

1. **feature** : characteristic.
2. **bizarre** : very strange and unusual.
3. **grotesque** : strange and unpleasant.
4. **mastermind** : genius.

The Bet

and two always equal four, except in unusual cases, when they may equal three or five. He believed that all things that start must go somewhere, and he was able to concentrate all the mental force of his ancestors to solve any problem.

The public knew Van Dusen as The Thinking Machine and perhaps this phrase described him best of all. He spent all his time in his small laboratory where he invented brilliant [1] theories that shocked scientists and had a profound [2] effect on the world.

END

The Thinking Machine didn't have many visitors. When people did come to see him they were usually scientists. Two of these men, Dr Charles Ransome and Alfred Fielding visited him one evening to discuss some theory (what it was exactly is of no importance).

"That is impossible," said Dr Ransome.

"Nothing is impossible," said The Thinking Machine. "The mind is master of all things. When science understands this, it will be a great day."

"What about the airship?" [3] asked Dr Ransome.

"That's not impossible at all," said The Thinking Machine. "It will be invented soon. I would do it myself, but unfortunately I'm too busy."

---

1. **brilliant** : highly skilled.
2. **profound** : deep or far-reaching.
3. **airship** : aircraft that consists of a large balloon filled with gas with a compartment for passengers.

The Problem of Cell 13

Dr Ransome laughed.

"I've heard you say things like that before," he said. "But they mean nothing. The mind may be master of the material world, but there are some problems that cannot be solved by thought alone."

"Give me an example," demanded The Thinking Machine.

Dr Ransome thought for a moment as he smoked. "Well, what about the walls of a prison?" he replied. "No man can escape from a cell just by thinking about it. If he could, there would be no

The Bet

prisoners." He continued. "Let's imagine a case. A cell for prisoners who are condemned to death. [1] These men will do anything to try to escape. Imagine you were in that cell. Could you escape?"

"Certainly," said The Thinking Machine.

"Of course," said Mr Fielding, "you could destroy the cell with an explosive, but if you are a prisoner inside the cell you can't have that."

---

1. **condemned to death** : punished with death penalty.

The Problem of Cell 13

"I don't need an explosive," said The Thinking Machine. "I would be just like any other prisoner and I would still be able to leave the cell."

"You could escape only if you entered it with tools," said Dr Ransome.

The Thinking Machine was visibly irritated. [1]

"Lock me in any cell in any prison anywhere at any time, wearing only normal clothes, and I'll escape in a week," he declared.

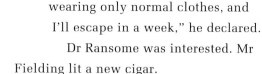

Dr Ransome was interested. Mr Fielding lit a new cigar.

"You're saying that you could escape from the cell just by thinking about it?" Ransome asked.

"I could get out."

"Are you serious?"

"Certainly, I'm serious."

Dr Ransome and Mr Fielding were silent for a long time.

"Would you like to try it?" asked Mr Fielding finally.

"Certainly," said Professor Van Dusen and added ironically, "I have done more ridiculous things than that to convince men of less important facts."

Of course it was an absurd thing but they decided it at that moment.

"To begin now," said Dr Ransome.

"I'd prefer tomorrow," said The Thinking Machine, "because ..."

"No, now!" said Mr Fielding. "You will be locked in a cell

---

1. **irritated** : annoyed.

The Bet

with no chance to communicate with friends. You will receive exactly the same attention as a real prisoner. A man condemned to death. Do you still agree to do it?"

"All right. Now, if you want," said The Thinking Machine, and he stood up.

"The death-cell in Chisholm Prison?"

"Fine."

"And what will you wear?"

"Very little," said The Thinking Machine. "Shoes, long socks, trousers and a shirt."

"The guards will search you, [1] of course."

"They must treat me like any other prisoner," said The Thinking Machine.

And so they made the arrangements. They had to obtain permission for the experiment but all three of them were important men and everything was finalised with a few telephone calls. The prison governors [2] could not understand why

---

1. **search you** : check that you have nothing hidden on you.
2. **prison governors** : people who manage the prison.

The Problem of Cell 13

Professor Van Dusen wanted to do it. But one thing was certain. They had never had such an important prisoner.

The Thinking Machine dressed himself in the clothes that he was going to wear in prison, and called his housekeeper.

"Martha," he said, "it is now twenty-seven minutes past nine. I am going away. One week from tonight at half-past nine, these gentlemen and one or two others will have dinner with me here. Remember Dr Ransome likes carrots."

A driver took the three men to Chisholm Prison. The warden [1] was waiting for them. He understood only that Professor Van Dusen was going to be his prisoner for one week. He was not a criminal, but he must be treated just like any other prisoner.

"Search him," said Dr Ransome.

The guards searched The Thinking Machine but they didn't find anything. The pockets of his trousers were empty and his shirt didn't have any pockets. They took off his shoes and socks and looked inside them. Nothing.

Dr Ransome regarded Van Dusen's weak body and his colourless face. He was suddenly sorry about his idea.

"Are you sure you want to do this?" he asked.

---

1. **warden** : supervisor of the prisoners.

The Bet

"Would you believe me if I didn't do it?" The Thinking Machine replied.

"No."

"All right, I'll do it."

Ransome didn't like the arrogance [1] in Van Dusen's voice. His sympathy [2] for the man disappeared. He decided that the experiment was a good thing. It would teach The Thinking Machine a lesson.

"Will it be possible for him to communicate with anyone outside the prison?" he asked.

"No. It will be absolutely impossible," said the warden. "He will not have anything to write with."

"And the guards, will they send messages for him?"

"Not one word," said the warden. "They will tell me anything he says and they will give me anything he gives them."

"Good," said Mr Fielding.

"Of course if he does not escape in a week," said Dr Ransome, "and asks to leave, you will let him go?"

"I understand," said the warden.

Then The Thinking Machine spoke.

"I have three requests," he said, "I would like some toothpaste and also one five-dollar and two ten-dollar bills. [3]"

"Could he bribe [4] your guards for twenty-five dollars?"

---

1. **arrogance** : a proud and superior manner.
2. **sympathy** : understanding and care.
3. **bills** : American English for paper money.
4. **bribe** : persuade someone to do something by offering money or services.

The Problem of Cell 13

"Not even for twenty-five hundred dollars."

"In that case, give him the money," said Mr Fielding.

"And what is the third request?" asked Dr Ransome.

"Could somebody clean my shoes?"

The three men looked very surprised. This last request seemed completely absurd, [1] but they agreed to it anyway. After this, they took The Thinking Machine to his cell. They walked down a long corridor and stopped at the third steel door.

"Here is Cell 13," said the warden. "This is where condemned killers are kept. No one can leave it without my permission. No one in it can communicate with

---

1. **absurd** : unreasonable, ridiculous.

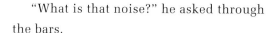

anyone outside. It is very near my office and I can hear any noise that comes from it."

"Is this cell all right, gentlemen?" asked The Thinking Machine.

"Yes, it's perfect," replied Fielding and Ransome together.

The guard opened the door and The Thinking Machine walked into the dark room. No sooner was he inside than the warden closed the door and locked it with a double lock. Ransome heard a noise from inside the cell.

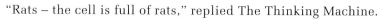

"What is that noise?" he asked through the bars.

"Rats – the cell is full of rats," replied The Thinking Machine.

The three men said goodnight and were turning to go when The Thinking Machine called:

"What time is it exactly, warden?"

"Seventeen minutes past eleven."

"Thanks. I will see you all in your office at half-past eight one week from this evening," said The Thinking Machine.

"And if you do not?"

"There is no possibility of that."

The Hero

1 These questions will help you to describe the main character of the story, Professor Augustus S.F.X. Van Dusen. Answer them and then write a paragraph describing him.

a. What did Professor Augustus S.F.X. Van Dusen look like?

b. Where was he originally from?

c. What was his real passion?

d. What was his nickname and why?

e. What did he do?

2 **Are these sentences true (T) or false (F)? Correct the false ones, as in the example.**

	T	F

a. The Thinking Machine was very outgoing.   ☐   F

The Thinking Machine hardly saw any people at all.

b. The Thinking Machine and his friends discussed issues concerning the material world and the mind.   ☐ ☐

c. Dr Ransome and Mr Fielding were very sceptical about The Thinking Machine's ideas.   ☐ ☐

d. Mr Fielding smoked cigarettes.   ☐ ☐

e. The Thinking Machine was supposed to wear shoes, short socks, trousers and a shirt for his experiment.   ☐ ☐

f. It was very difficult to obtain permission for the experiment.   ☐ ☐

g. Dr Ransome felt very sorry about the fact that The Thinking Machine would have to spend some time in prison like a real prisoner.   ☐ ☐

h. The warden reassured Ransome and Fielding that they would be very strict with their new prisoner.   ☐ ☐

i. The Thinking Machine was likely to succeed in bribing the guards.   ☐ ☐

j. Cell 13 was where they kept condemned killers.   ☐ ☐

k. The Thinking Machine had to make his escape within one week.   ☐ ☐

Prediction

3 **The Thinking Machine had three requests:**

- some toothpaste
- one five-dollar and two ten-dollar bills
- to have his shoes cleaned

Can you think of some reasons for this?

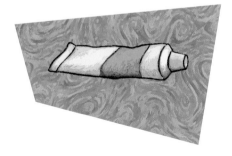

Third Conditional

4 **The Thinking Machine went to his cell with a few things. Imagine he had brought the following things: what could he have done?**

a. a gun If he had brought a gun, he could have ....

b. a saw ....

c. a notebook ....

d. a tape recorder ....

e. a rope ....

f. a pair of handcuffs ....

Reported Speech

5 **Rewrite the following sentences and change them into reported speech.**

a. "That is impossible," said Dr Ransome to The Thinking Machine.
....

b. "I've heard you say things like that before," he said.
....

c. "I don't need an explosive," said The Thinking Machine.
....

d. "Are you serious?" he asked.
....

e. "And what will you wear?" he asked.
....

f. "Could he bribe your guards for twenty-five dollars?" he asked.
....

OTHER PRISON STORIES

One of the things that makes *The Problem of Cell 13* so interesting is that it combines elements of the detective story (the solution of a "locked room" mystery) with the drama of a daring [1] escape. And here the detective and the "criminal" are the same person. The Thinking Machine's detection of the solution paradoxically [2] constitutes his "crime" of escaping from prison. But Van Dusen's escape has many precedents both in literature and in life. The most famous of all prison escape stories is of course Alexandre Dumas's *The Count of*

Alexandre Dumas.

Monte Cristo in which the wrongly imprisoned hero Edmond Dantès, escapes by substituting himself with the body of another prisoner, recently deceased [3] – his friend the Abbé Faria. The guards

Le Château d'If from which Dantès escaped in *The Count of Monte Cristo*.

---

1. **daring** : brave and taking risks.
2. **paradoxically** : in a contradictory way.
3. **deceased** : dead.

throw what they believe to be the Abbé's body, closed in a sack, into the sea and Dantès, after freeing himself, swims to the surface and is picked up by a boat.

A true escape story that was, like many other episodes [1] of his life, undoubtedly exaggerated [2] by its author was that of Giovanni Giacomo Casanova, who escaped from a Venetian prison, assisted by a monk called Balbi. Apparently, Casanova asked a guard to deliver a bowl of macaroni and a bible to the monk. The guard was so busy trying not to spill the macaroni that he did not notice the unusual weight of the bible which had been hollowed out [3] to accommodate [4] a metal spike. Balbi then used the spike to dig a hole in the prison roof.

A portrait of G. G. Casanova.

The Ponte dei Sospiri; the entrance to the Venetian Prison where Casanova was imprisoned.

More recently, the theme of escape has inspired some wonderful films, the most notable being, Mervin LeRoy's *I am a Fugitive from a Chain Gang*,

---

1. **episodes** : parts of a story.
2. **exaggerated** : made to seem larger or better than it really was.
3. **bible ... hollowed out** : the inside part of the bible had been removed.
4. **accommodate** : provide with a place to be stored in.

The entrance to Alcatraz.

The Island of Alcatraz.

1932, whose hero ends up back in prison years after his original escape; Don Seigel's *Escape from Alcatraz*, 1979, about the only man ever believed to have escaped from the famous island prison; and French director Robert Bresson's masterpiece *Un Condamné à mort s'est echappé*, 1956, *(A Man Escaped)* in which escape becomes almost a religious quest [1] for the protagonist, [2] a French resistance fighter condemned to death by the Nazis.

The theme of escape is one that continues to fascinate us. Its appeal to writers and film directors inevitably has something to do with the fact that escaping from prison, like writing, requires a great deal of imagination. As the narrator of Italo Calvino's modern version of *The Count of Monte Cristo* says: "If I succeed in mentally constructing a fortress from

---

1. **quest** : an attempt to achieve something difficult.
2. **protagonist** : the most important character of a story.

which it is impossible to escape, this conceived [1] fortress either will be the same as the real one – and in this case it is certain we shall never escape from here [...] or it will be a fortress from which escape is even more impossible than from here – and this, then, is a sign that here an opportunity of escape exists: we have only to identify the point where the imagined fortress does not coincide with the real one and then find it."

The cells of Alcatraz.

1 **Now answer the following questions:**

   a. How did the hero of *The Count of Monte Cristo* manage to escape?

   b. What did Balbi use to dig a hole in the prison roof? Where did he get it?

   c. What is the film *Escape from Alcatraz* about? What makes its story unique?

   d. Who directed *A Man Escaped*? When is it set?

   e. Why does the theme of escape fascinate us so much?

   f. In what way is being in prison similar to writing?

---

1. **conceived** : imaginary.

CHAPTER TWO

Chisholm Prison

C hisholm prison was a large building. It was four floors high and stood in the centre of a large open space. The wall around it was six metres high and impossible to climb. Even if a man managed to escape from his cell, he could not pass over the wall.

The yard [1] around the building was eight metres wide on all sides. This was the distance from the prison building to the wall. During the day, prisoners used the yard to do exercises. But it was not for those prisoners in Cell 13.

There were always four armed guards in the yard, one for each side of the building.

At night strong lights illuminated [2] the yard and the wall. The

---

1. **yard** : flat enclosed area of concrete or stone.
2. **illuminated** : made something brighter.

wires that carried electricity to these lights ran up the walls of the building.

The Thinking Machine saw and understood all these things. He had to stand on his bed to see out of the small barred window. It was the morning after his incarceration. [1] He soon realised that somewhere on the other side of the wall there was a river because he could hear the sound of a boat and saw a river bird in the sky. From the same direction he heard the sound of children playing baseball, so he knew that there was a children's playground between the prison wall and the river.

No man had ever escaped from Chisholm Prison and it was easy to see why. The walls of the cell were perfectly solid and the bars on the window were new. And in any case the window itself was too small to escape through.

But this didn't discourage The Thinking Machine. He looked up at the light and saw how the wire went from it to the wall of the prison building. He realised that the wire passed near the window of his cell. That could be useful.

Cell 13 was on the same floor as the prison offices. The Thinking Machine couldn't see the ground through the window of his cell. However, there were only four steps up to the office floor. Therefore the cell must be near the ground. Good.

The Thinking Machine remembered how he had come to the

---

1. **incarceration** : the keeping of someone in prison.

cell. First there was the outside guard's room which formed part of the wall, next to the prison gates. There was always one guard at these gates who let people come into the prison and then let them out again when the warden told him to. The warden's office was in the prison building. From the yard you had to pass through a solid steel door to get to it. The door had only one small hole in it

to see who was there. Then between the office and Cell 13 there was a heavy wooden door and two steel doors in the corridors of the prison. Then, of course, there was the door of Cell 13.

"There are seven doors between Cell 13 and freedom," thought The Thinking Machine. "It will not be easy. But there are advantages. I am alone here. Nobody looks at what I am doing.

The Problem of Cell 13

There is one guard who brings my food three times a day, at six o'clock in the morning, at noon, then again at six in the afternoon. And then there is the inspection at nine o'clock. But that is all."

There was nothing, absolutely nothing in his cell except a bed that was strongly made and impossible to dismantle. [1] There was no chair, no table, no cup or fork or spoon. Nothing. The guard watched him while he ate and took away his plate and spoon as soon as he had finished.

The Thinking Machine considered all these facts very carefully. Then he began an examination of his cell. He examined the stones in the walls and roof and the cement between them. He walked over the floor many times but it was solid cement. After the examination he sat on his bed and thought for a long time. Because Professor Augustus S.F.X. Van Dusen had something to think about.

Suddenly, he was disturbed by a rat which ran across his foot and disappeared into a dark corner of the cell. The Thinking Machine looked hard into the corner. After some time he saw several pairs of yellow eyes looking back at him.

Then for the first time The Thinking Machine noticed the bottom of his cell door. There was a space of about five centimetres between the steel bar and the floor. The Thinking Machine walked into the corner where the rats were, but he

---

1. **dismantle** : (here) take his bed to pieces.

continued to look at the door. The rats were afraid and tried to escape. There was the sound of running feet and several squeaks [1] and then silence.

None of the rats had gone out the door, yet the cell was now empty. Therefore there must be another way out of the cell, even if it was

very small. He got down on his hands and knees and began to look for the opening. Finally he found it. It was a small circular hole in the floor about four centimetres in diameter. "So this is how the rats escaped. Interesting." He put his hand in the hole. It seemed to be an old drainpipe. [2]

The Thinking Machine sat on the bed and thought for an hour. Then he looked once more outside his cell window. One of the outside guards stood directly opposite, beside the wall. He was looking at the window of Cell 13 when The Thinking Machine's large head appeared. But the Professor didn't see the guard.

At twelve o'clock the Cell 13 guard brought The Thinking Machine his food. It was horrible but The Thinking Machine didn't mind. He wasn't interested in food. He spoke to the guard, who watched him as he ate.

"Have they made any modifications [3] here in the last few years?" asked The Thinking Machine.

---

1. **squeaks** : sounds made by rats.
2. **drainpipe** : tube through which rain or dirty water runs.
3. **modifications** : changes.

"Not really," said the guard. "They built the new wall four years ago."

"Have they done anything to the prison building?"

"Well, they painted the outside. And then seven years ago they had a new plumbing [1] system installed."

"Ah, I see," said the prisoner. "How far is the river over there?"

"About a hundred metres. The boys have a baseball ground between the wall and the river."

The Thinking Machine had nothing more to say, but when the guard was ready to go he asked for some water.

"I get very thirsty here," he explained. "Could I have some water in a cup please?"

"I'll ask the warden," replied the guard, and he went away.

Half an hour later he returned with a small cup.

"The warden says you may keep this cup," he told the prisoner. "But you must show it to me when I ask for it. If you break it, I won't give you another one."

"Thank you," said The Thinking Machine. "I won't break it."

Two hours later the same guard was passing the door of Cell 13. He heard a noise and stopped. The Thinking Machine was on his hands and knees in a corner of the cell. There was the sound of several squeaks. The guard watched him.

---

1. **plumbing** : water supply.

Chisholm Prison

"Ah, I've got you," he heard the prisoner say.

"What have you got?" said the guard.

"One of these rats," he replied. "See?" The guard saw a rat in The Thinking Machine's hands. The prisoner carried it towards the light. "It's a water rat," he said.

"Haven't you got anything better to do than catch rats?" asked the guard.

"It's terrible that there are rats in this prison," said The Thinking Machine. "Take this one away and kill it. There are many more where it came from."

The guard took the rat and killed it. Later he told the warden about the incident, but the warden only smiled.

Later that afternoon the armed guard in the yard outside Cell 13 saw the prisoner look out and put a hand through the bars of the window. Something white fell slowly to the ground. It was a roll of linen from a shirt, and wrapped [1] around it was a five-dollar bill. The guard looked up at the window again but the face was no longer there.

With a smile he took the cloth and the five-dollar bill to the warden's office. There was something written on the outside of the cloth in strange ink. It said:

"Please deliver [2] to Dr Charles Ransome."

---

1. **wrapped** : (here) tied.
2. **deliver** : take.

"Ha!" said the warden, "His first plan of escape has failed. But why did he address it to Dr Ransome?"

"And where did he get the pen and ink to write with?" added the guard.

The warden looked at the guard and the guard looked at the warden. There was no easy solution to the mystery. The warden studied the writing carefully.

"Well, let's see what he wanted to say to Dr Ransome," he said. He unrolled the second piece of linen.

" Well, if that – what – what do you think of that?" he asked, extremely confused.

The guard took the piece of linen and read:

"Epa cseot d'net niiy awe htto n'si sih. T."

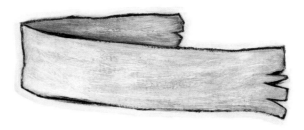

1 **What happened in Chapter Two? Answer the following questions.**

a. What kinds of noises did The Thinking Machine hear from his cell?

b. Where was the cell exactly?

c. Despite the terrible conditions in the cell, The Thinking Machine found there were some advantages to his position. What were they?

d. Was the cell furnished?

e. What did he find at the bottom of the cell door?

f. Had there been any modifications made to the prison lately?

g. What was between the river and the wall?

h. What did he give to the guard?

i. Why were the guard and the warden surprised?

Chisholm Prison – test your memory

2 Listen to the description of the prison. There are eight differences from the original. Listen once. Pause to take notes. Listen again. Write down as many differences as you can.

1. ....

2. ....

3. ....

4. ....

5. ....

6. ....

7. ....

8. ....

Prediction

3 **The story is getting more and more mysterious. Try to work out the following problems:**

   a. Where did The Thinking Machine find the cloth to wrap the money around?

   b. What did he use to write?

   c. EPA CSEOT D'NET NIIY AWE HTTO N'SI SIH. T.
Is this some kind of exotic language? But The Thinking Machine was not a polyglot. Can you work out what it means?

Materials

4 **Find at least three things that are made of:**

   a. wire ....

   b. steel ....

   c. wood ....

   d. stone ....

   e. cement ....

   f. cloth ....

The Passive

5 **Rewrite the following sentences in the passive form.**

   a. But this didn't discourage The Thinking Machine.

   ....

   ....

   b. There is one guard who brings my food here three times a day.

   ....

   ....

   c. They had told the guard to watch him when he ate.

   ....

   ....

   d. If a rat hadn't disturbed The Thinking Machine, he wouldn't have found the opening.

   ....

   ....

   e. The warden saw that he had written a message on the linen.

   ....

   ....

   f. The electricity company was going to install a new lighting system.

   ....

   ....

Summary

6 **Read the summary of the first two chapters and fill in the gaps with the words from the box.**

invents	message	three	world	window	bet
theory	freedom	yard	condemned	drainpipe	
Machine	escape	rats	permission	cleans	walls

Professor Van Dusen is known as The Thinking [1]..................... . Logic is his passion, and he [2]..................... brilliant theories that have a profound effect on the [3]..................... .

One evening while he is discussing some [4]..................... with his two friends, Dr Ransome and Mr Fielding, he makes a [5]..................... with them that if he were locked in a prison cell, he would be able to [6]..................... in a week.

After obtaining [7]..................... for the experiment, they go to Chisolm Prison where Van Dusen is searched. The Thinking Machine asks for [8]..................... things: some toothpaste, one five-dollar and two ten-dollar bills, and that somebody [9]..................... his shoes. They agree to his requests and then he is locked in Cell 13, the cell for [10]..................... killers.

The Thinking Machine studies his prison cell carefully – Chisolm Prison seems to be impossible to escape from; the prison [11]..................... are six metres high, there are four armed guards in the [12]..................... and there are seven locked doors between Cell 13 and [13]..................... .

There is nothing in his cell except for a bed that is impossible to dismantle and [14]..................... which disappear into a hole in the corner of the cell, which The Thinking Machine discovers is an old [15]..................... .

Later that afternoon the armed guard in the yard outside Cell 13 sees something fall from the [16]..................... . It is a roll of linen from a shirt and wrapped around it is a five-dollar bill. Written on the linen is a strange [17].....................: "Epa cseot d'net niiy awe htto n'si sih. T."

Before you read

1 **Listen Carefully!**

Listen to the first part of Chapter Three and fill in the gaps with the correct word.

The 1......................... spent an hour trying to 2......................... what the message was. Why did his 3......................... want to talk to Dr Ransome? And where had he 4......................... the materials to write? He examined the 5......................... again. It was a part of a white shirt. But what had he written 6.........................? The warden knew that the prisoner didn't have a pen or a pencil. So what had he used? The warden 7......................... to investigate. The Thinking Machine was his prisoner. "If this man is trying to 8......................... by sending 9......................... messages," he thought, "I will stop him."

The warden 10......................... to Cell 13. He found The Thinking Machine on his hands and 11......................... . He was 12......................... rats. The prisoner 13......................... the warden and turned to him 14......................... .

Now read and check if you were right!

CHAPTER THREE

A Message from Cell 13

The warden spent an hour trying to discover what the message was. Why did his prisoner want to talk to Dr Ransome? And where had he got the materials to write? He examined the linen again. It was a part of a white shirt. But what had he written with? The warden knew that the prisoner didn't have a pen or a pencil. So what had he used? The warden decided to investigate. The Thinking Machine was his prisoner. "If this man is trying to escape by sending coded messages," he thought, "I will stop him."

The warden returned to Cell 13. He found The Thinking Machine on his hands and knees. He was catching rats. The prisoner heard the warden and turned to him quickly.

END

44

"It's terrible," he said. "These rats. There are hundreds of them."

"Other men can live with them," said the warden. "Give me your shirt. Here is another one."

"Why?" demanded The Thinking Machine.

"You have attempted to communicate with Dr Ransome," said the warden, angrily. "As the warden of this prison, I must stop you." The Thinking Machine was silent for a moment.

"All right," he said, finally. "Here. Take it."

The warden smiled. The prisoner stood up and took off his shirt. He gave it to the warden. In exchange, the warden gave him a blue prison shirt. The warden looked at The Thinking Machine's white shirt. He compared the pieces of linen he had with the shirt. It was torn in two places. The Thinking Machine watched him.

"Did the guard give you those?" he asked.

"Yes, he did," said the warden. "And that is the end of your first attempt to escape." The Thinking Machine watched the warden as he looked at the shirt. He saw that there were only two pieces missing from it. He smiled.

"What did you write this message with?" asked the warden.

"I'm afraid *you* must discover that!" The Thinking Machine said.

The warden became angry but he didn't say anything more. He made a very careful inspection of the cell and the prisoner, but he found nothing. Nothing that The Thinking Machine could use as a pen. And the liquid that he had used to write the message was also a mystery. Finally the warden went out of the cell. He took The Thinking Machine's shirt with him.

"Well, he won't escape by writing messages on a shirt," the warden thought.

On the third day of his incarceration The Thinking Machine tried to bribe the guard so that he could escape. The guard brought his food and waited outside the cell door.

"The drainpipes of the prison go to the river, don't they?" The Thinking Machine asked.

"Yes," said the guard.

"I imagine they are very small?"

"Yes. They are too small to escape through."

There was silence. The Thinking Machine finished his food. Then he said:

"You know I'm not a criminal, don't you?"

"Yes."

"And I can leave the prison if I want to?"

"Yes."

"Well, when I came here I believed I could escape," said the prisoner. "Will you help me if I give you some money?"

The guard was an honest man.

"No," he said.

The Problem of Cell 13

"Five hundred dollars," said The Thinking Machine. "I am not a criminal."

"No," said the guard.

"A thousand?"

"No. If you gave me ten thousand dollars, I couldn't get you out. To get out you have to pass through seven doors and I only have the keys to two."

The guard ran to the warden's office and told him about the prisoner's offer.

"Plan number two fails," said the warden and smiled. "First a message and then a bribe."

At six o'clock, the guard went to Cell 13 again to bring food to The Thinking Machine. He stopped in the corridor. There was a noise coming from inside the cell. The guard walked very quietly to the cell door. Through the bars he saw The Thinking Machine at the window. He was trying to cut through the iron bars of the window with a file. [1]

The guard went back to the office and told the warden. The two men went back to Cell 13, walking very quietly. The warden looked into the cell and saw The Thinking Machine still at the window. He entered the cell.

The Thinking Machine turned round and jumped onto the floor. He tried to hide the file in his hand.

---

1. **file** : instrument used to cut through metal.

A Message from Cell 13

"Give it to me," said the warden.

"No," said the prisoner. There was anger in his voice.

"Come on. Give it to me."

"No," repeated The Thinking Machine.

"Very well. Search him," said the warden to the guard.

The guard searched The Thinking Machine. After some minutes he found a piece of steel about five centimetres long in the prisoner's trousers. A few minutes later he found another piece. The guard gave the pieces of steel to the warden. The warden looked at them.

"You couldn't cut through the bars on the window with these," he said.

"Yes I could," said The Thinking Machine.

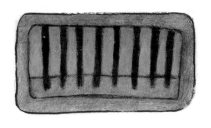

"In six months perhaps," said the warden, smiling.

"Just wait, you'll see," said The Thinking Machine.

Once more the guard searched the cell. But once more they found nothing.

The warden stood on the bed and looked at the bars of the window. He took the bars in his hand and tried to move them. They were immovable. He smiled and then got down from the bed.

"Forget it, Professor, you will never escape from here," he said.

The Thinking Machine said nothing. He just sat on the bed with his head in his hands. The warden and the guard went out of the cell and closed the door.

The Problem of Cell 13

"He is mad to try and escape," said the warden, "but he is very clever. I would like to know what he used to write that coded message."

It was four o'clock the next morning when a terrible scream resounded [1] through the prison. It came from a cell near the centre of the building, a sound full of horror and great fear. The warden heard it and ran with three of his men into the long corridor that went to Cell 13.

---

1. **resounded** : sounded loudly.

Unfinished Sentences

1 **Complete the following sentences with the right pieces of information. (They follow the order of the story.)**

a. The warden wanted the prisoner to

  ....

b. The warden became angry because he couldn't understand

  ....

c. On the third day of his incarceration, The Thinking Machine tried to

  ....

d. The guard refused, partly because he had only

  ....

e. At six o'clock the guard saw the prisoner while he was

  ....

f. When the guard searched the prisoner he found

  ....

g. At four o'clock the next morning the warden heard

  ....

Rats

2 **"It's terrible," he said. "These rats. There are hundreds of them."**

a. Are you afraid of rats?

b. What are the things that scare you most?

c. What's the scariest thing you've ever seen? (This could be from a horror movie or even from a real experience.)

Prediction

3 **The enigma is getting stranger. Try to predict the following mysteries.**

    a. Where did The Thinking Machine find the pieces of steel?

    b. What was the scream the warden heard?

    c. Why was the man screaming?

Past Perfect

4 At four o'clock a terrible scream resounded through the prison... but a lot of other bizarre things had happened before.

Use the cues to write complete sentences to recall the strange events which had taken place in Chisholm Prison before that morning. (Remember to use the Past Perfect!)

Before that morning:

    a. The Thinking Machine – give a piece of cloth

    b. the warden – try to interpret the message

    c. The Thinking Machine – find lots of rats

    d. the warden – take The Thinking Machine's shirt

    e. The Thinking Machine – try to bribe

    f. The Thinking Machine – attempt to cut

Discipline in a Prison

5 Use the expressions below to make sentences about prison life as in the example.

a. had to *In the past, prisoners had to work on the railroad.*

b. have to ....

c. are allowed to ....

d. aren't allowed to ....

e. mustn't ....

f. don't have to ....

g. shouldn't ....

h. needn't ....

i. should ....

j. can ....

Time for thinking

6 **a.** Is discipline important to you?

b. In which jobs is it important to have discipline?

c. "Children need to be disciplined." What do you think?

d. Do you believe in the "carrot and stick" method? Why/Why not?

7 **Can you find seven hidden words connected with the idea of mystery?**

P	M	S	T	R	A	N	G	E	D
D	U	D	M	Y	M	X	B	Z	W
G	R	Z	Z	U	G	J	T	T	S
L	D	H	Z	R	I	D	D	L	E
S	E	Q	G	L	N	K	J	G	C
E	R	S	Y	W	E	I	R	D	R
A	R	H	P	E	Q	K	K	S	E
D	I	L	E	M	M	A	P	S	T
Q	N	M	M	P	L	S	F	H	J
F	M	S	A	K	L	C	X	Z	S

FUTRELLE'S DEATH ON THE TITANIC

Not much is known about Futrelle's life but we can imagine a lot about his death. Jacques Futrelle was a passenger on the *Titanic* and was one of the 1,503 people who lost their lives after the ship collided with an iceberg. The "Ship of Dreams" sank in the early hours of April 15, 1912. It was, many said, the end of an epoch, [1] a farewell to the age of travel in the grand style.

The *Titanic* was laid down [2] on March 31, 1909 and was launched on May 31, 1911. She had nine decks and was designed to remain afloat [3] with any two compartments flooded, possibly three, enabling her to resist a collision at the joint of two compartments.

The British Board of Regulations required that any ship over 10,000 tons had to carry sixteen

Titanic in White Star Dock, painted by G. Fraser.

---

1. **epoch** : a long period of time.
2. **laid down** : construction began.
3. **afloat** : floating on water.

lifeboats. As the *Titanic* carried 20 lifeboats she was well within the regulations. In fact, no liner afloat at that time carried enough lifeboats to evacuate [1] all passengers and crew. The Board briefly considered raising the legal minimum to 32 but decided against it. Her overall length was 882 feet 6 inches, her beam [2] was 92 feet 6 inches and she was 60 feet 6 inches from water line to boat deck. Her net tonnage was of 24,900 tons.

On April 2, 1912 the completed ship set sail from Belfast for her sea trials. No one could have known that in less than two weeks she would be 12,500 feet down at the bottom of the Atlantic Ocean, her

Second-class passengers on the boat deck.

---

1. **evacuate** : move people from a dangerous place to a safe place.
2. **beam** : the widest part of a ship.

hull [1] cleft [2] in two. On the contrary, the "Olympic Class" liners were widely regarded as unsinkable. They had no need of lifeboats for they were themselves "lifeboats."

But when the ship hit an iceberg on April 15, 1912, the ship's designer Thomas Andrews did not take long to confirm that she could not survive the damage caused by the collision and would inevitably sink within a few hours.

She took less than three hours to sink. At the beginning most passengers were unaware of the seriousness of the incident or even that a

Thomas Andrews,
the ship's designer.

collision had occurred. But as she began listing [3] more heavily, a number of passengers became quite willing to climb aboard the ship's lifeboats. The ship's officers, however, were at first reluctant [4] to fill the boats, thinking they would break under the stress of a full load. Thus, although they had been designed to accommodate up to seventy people, many of the lifeboats were lowered into the sea less than half-full.

The *Titanic*'s condition progressively worsened as the bow sank lower and lower. With all the lifeboats gone, the remaining 1,503 passengers

---

1. **hull** : main body of the ship.
2. **cleft** : (infin. cleave) broken, split.
3. **listing** : leaning over on one side.
4. **reluctant** : unwilling.

A first-class bedroom.

Captain Smith,
the commander
of the *Titanic*.

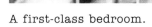

A second-class
breakfast menu.

The Café Parisien, *Titanic*.

The gymnasium.

The telegraph room.

A private terrace
of a suite.

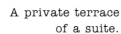

Lifeboats on the promenade [1] deck.

1. **promenade** : a walking path next to the sea, where people can walk for pleasure.

must have started to come to terms with their fate. Among them was Jacques Futrelle. Not even the ingenuity [1] of his Thinking Machine could help him now. Futrelle went down with the ship while his wife survived, one of the lucky ones who had managed to secure herself a place on a lifeboat.

Survivors of the disaster reported many acts of nobility and selfless heroism amidst the general panic. We know that the ship's orchestra continued to play throughout the entire ordeal [2] and that they were still playing as the ship went under at 2.20 am on April 15, 1912.

1 **Are these sentences true (T) or false (F)? Correct the false ones.**

		T	F
a.	Both Futrelle and his wife died during the sinking of the *Titanic*.	☐	☐
b.	The *Titanic* was launched on May 31st, 1911.	☐	☐
c.	The *Titanic* carried 32 lifeboats.	☐	☐
d.	Her overall length was 882.5 feet.	☐	☐
e.	She took less than two hours to sink.	☐	☐
f.	Most passengers were very alarmed because they immediately realised what was happening.	☐	☐
g.	The ship's designer was one of the passengers.	☐	☐
h.	The ship's orchestra died along with the other passengers who didn't manage to get into a lifeboat.	☐	☐

---

1. **ingenuity** : ability to think of clever ways of doing something.
2. **ordeal** : (here) a terrible experience.

2 Answer the following questions.

a. How many people lost their lives on the *Titanic*?

....

b. How many decks did the liner have?

....

c. Why was the *Titanic* considered "unsinkable"?

....

d. From where did the *Titanic* leave for her sea trials?

....

e. What was the name of the ship's designer?

....

f. How many people were the lifeboats designed to accommodate?

....

g. Why were many of the lifeboats less than half full?

....

Titanic by Walter Dane Bryer, 1912.

Before you read

1 Below are the first 6 paragraphs of Chapter Four. Try to fill in the gaps using the words from the box and then put the paragraphs in their correct order. Now listen to the CD to check your answers.

child	heard	white	Ballard	acid
wrong	warden	take	scream	
above	crazy	crying	prove	

a. ☐ "What's 1......................?" demanded the warden.
"Thank God you've come," said the prisoner.
"What is it?" demanded the warden again.
He opened the door and went into Cell 43. The prisoner's face was 2...................... with terror.

b. ☐ He stopped and looked into the cell. "That 3......................
man in Cell 13" was sleeping comfortably in his bed. They heard the scream again. It was coming from somewhere 4...................... . The warden and the guards went upstairs. There they found a man in Cell 43, directly above Cell 13. He was sitting in the corner of his cell like a 5...................... .

c. ☐ "Who is this man?" the warden asked the guard.
"His name is Joseph 6......................," the guard replied.
"And what is his crime?"
"They say he killed a woman with 7...................... ."

d. ☐ As they ran they heard the [8]..................... again. The white faces of prisoners appeared at cell doors. They were afraid. "It's that crazy man in Cell 13," the [9]..................... said.

e. ☐ "But they can't prove it," said the prisoner. "They can't [10]..................... it!"

The warden was silent for a minute.

"Listen to me, Ballard," he said, finally. "If you heard something, I want to know what it was. Now tell me."

"I can't tell you." Ballard was [11]..................... now.

"Where did it come from?"

"I don't know. Everywhere – nowhere. I don't know."

f. ☐ "Take me out of this cell, please take me out," he said.

"What is it?" asked the warden.

"I [12]..................... something – something."

"What did you hear?"

"I can't tell you," said the prisoner. "Please [13].....................
me out of this cell – put me anywhere – but take me out of here."

CHAPTER FOUR

A Strange Voice

As they ran they heard the scream again. The white faces of prisoners appeared at cell doors. They were afraid.

"It's that crazy man in Cell 13," the warden said.

He stopped and looked into the cell. "That crazy man in Cell 13" was sleeping comfortably in his bed. They heard the scream again. It was coming from somewhere above. The warden and the guards went upstairs. There they found a man in Cell 43, directly above Cell 13. He was sitting in the corner of his cell like a child.

"What's wrong?" demanded the warden.

"Thank God you've come," said the prisoner.

"What is it?" demanded the warden again.

He opened the door and went into Cell 43. The prisoner's face was white with terror.

"Take me out of this cell, please take me out," he said.

"What is it?" asked the warden.

"I heard something – something."

"What did you hear?"

"I can't tell you," said the prisoner. "Please take me out of this cell – put me anywhere – but take me out of here."

"Who is this man?" the warden asked the guard.

"His name is Joseph Ballard," the guard replied.

"And what is his crime?"

"They say he killed a woman with acid."

"But they can't prove it," said the prisoner. "They can't prove it!"

The warden was silent for a minute.

"Listen to me, Ballard," he said, finally. "If you heard something, I want to know what it was. Now tell me."

"I can't tell you." Ballard was crying now.

"Where did it come from?"

"I don't know. Everywhere – nowhere. I don't know."

"Was it a voice?"

"I can't tell you," said the prisoner.

"You must tell me," said the warden, angrily.

"It was a voice – but – but – it wasn't human," said the prisoner.

"A voice, but not human?" repeated the warden. He was confused.

"It was strange and very far away, like a ghost."

"Did it come from inside or outside the prison?"

"It didn't come from anywhere. It was here, there, everywhere. I heard it. I heard it!"

A Strange Voice

For an hour the warden tried to get the story, but Ballard became silent and didn't say anything more. Finally the warden went away. He was very confused. Ballard sat at his cell door until morning, his white face staring through the bars.

It was the fourth day of The Thinking Machine's incarceration. He stood at his cell window and threw another piece of linen to the guard outside. And once more the guard took it to the warden. The warden read the message on it. It said:

"Only three days more."

The warden was not surprised by the message. He knew The Thinking Machine meant that there were only three days more before he escaped.

"But how did he write it?" the warden thought. "Where did he find another piece of linen? Where? How?" He looked at the linen. It was white, like the material from a shirt. He took The Thinking Machine's shirt and put the two original pieces of linen on the torn places. The third piece was completely superfluous. [1] But it was the same material. "Where did he get it? And where – where does he get anything to write with?"

Later on the fourth day The Thinking Machine spoke to the guard outside his window.

"What day of the month is it?" he asked.

"The fifteenth."

The Thinking Machine made a mental astronomical [2] calculation. "Good," he thought. "Tonight the moon will not rise before nine o'clock." Then he asked another question.

"Who looks after the big lights on the roof?"

---

1. **superfluous** : more than is needed.
2. **astronomical** : scientific.

"An electrician from the company."

"You have no electricians in the building?"

"No."

At the end of the afternoon, just before he finished work, the outside guard saw The Thinking Machine's head again at the window. He had something in his hand which he threw to the ground. It was a five-dollar bill.

"That's for you," said the prisoner.

Once again, the guard took it to the warden.

"He said it was for me."

"I imagine it's a present from him. I think you can accept it," said the warden. Then suddenly he stopped. "Wait a minute. When the professor went into the cell he had one five-dollar bill and two ten-dollar bills. There was a five-dollar bill with the first message. I have it here. But now he has given you another five-dollar bill. It's impossible. He has only two ten-dollar bills."

"Perhaps somebody changed a ten-dollar bill for him," said the guard.

"Perhaps. But tonight we are going to search Cell 13 again. We are going to search it as no cell has ever been searched before."

So that night at three o'clock in the morning the warden and his guards searched The Thinking Machine's cell again. The warden found the hole in the floor. He put his hand into it. There was something there. He pulled it out. A dead rat. He threw it to the floor in disgust. But he continued the search. Once more he examined the bars on the window but found them to be solid. He then examined The Thinking Machine's clothes. In his trousers he found some money.

"Five one-dollar bills!" said the warden. He was very surprised.

"That's right," said the prisoner.

"But the … you had two tens and a five … how do you do it?"

"That's my business," said The Thinking Machine.

"Did any of my men change this money for you?"

"No."

"Well, do you make it?" asked the warden.

"That's my business," said the prisoner again.

The warden was very angry. He left the cell and went back to bed.

About an hour later he heard the scream again. He got up and ran immediately to Cell 43, where he saw Ballard, his terrorised face pressed against the bars of the door.

"Take me out, take me out," he screamed. "I did it. I did it. I killed her. Take me out of here."

"Was it the voice again?" asked the warden.

"Yes," said Ballard.

"What did it say?"

"Acid – acid – acid!" said the prisoner. "It knew. I threw the acid in the woman's face and killed her. Oh!"

"Acid?" repeated the warden, more confused than ever.

Ballard

1 The prisoner Ballard murdered his girlfriend but we don't know much about him. Look at the pictures below, they can help you to recount the story of his life. Write a paragraph about his actions in the week before the murder.

every day

Monday

Tuesday

Wednesday

Thursday

Friday

2 **Are these sentences true (T) or false (F)? Correct the false ones.**

		T	F
a.	When the warden went to Cell 13 he found The Thinking Machine screaming.	☐	☐
b.	The prisoner Ballard was scared because he saw a strange shadow in his cell resembling a ghost.	☐	☐
c.	The Thinking Machine passed the guard another piece of cloth with a message on it.	☐	☐
d.	The message was again written in a secret code.	☐	☐
e.	The Thinking Machine tried to bribe the guard again with a ten-dollar bill.	☐	☐
f.	The warden and the guard found a hole in the floor with a dead rat in it.	☐	☐
g.	Ballard confessed to killing the woman because he repeatedly heard a voice shouting her name.	☐	☐

Prediction

3 **a.** How did The Thinking Machine get hold of the five-dollar bill, since he didn't have it when he entered Cell 13?

b. Why did he give it to the guard? It can't have been just a present.

c. We know the words: "Acid-acid-acid". Who was shouting? Why?

Letter

4 **Imagine you are Joseph Ballard. Write a letter to your friend Bill describing what is going on in prison and why you are so scared.**

Relative Clauses

5 **Link the two sentences with a relative pronoun. Omit it when you can!**

a. The prisoner Ballard confessed to murdering the woman. He thought he heard voices coming from the pipes.

b. The warden and the guard went to the cell. They had locked The Thinking Machine in it.

c. The Thinking Machine gave the guard a piece of linen. There was a message on it.

d. The message said "Only three days more". The guard showed it to the warden.

e. The Thinking Machine was very good at mathematics. He calculated that the moon that night wouldn't have risen before night o'clock.

f. The voice scared Ballard. It sounded like a ghost.

g. The warden and the guard searched The Thinking Machine's cell again. They were really furious about what was happening.

Past Perfect Continuous

6 **Imagine the characters' moods and feelings and answer the following questions.**

a. The warden looked fed up. What had he been doing?

b. The Thinking Machine looked exhausted. What had he been doing?

c. Dr Ransome and Mr Fielding looked worried. What had they been doing?

d. Ballard looked frightened. What had he been doing?

e. The guard looked puzzled. What had he been doing?

Summary

7 **Read the summary and fill in the gaps using the verbs in brackets. Put them in the correct form, using either the affirmative or negative.**

The warden ¹............................ *(can)* understand the strange message and how the prisoner ²............................ *(write)* it as he ³............................ *(have)* a pen or pencil. He ⁴............................ *(go)* to Cell 13 ⁵............................ *(investigate)* and ⁶............................ *(find)* The Thinking Machine ⁷............................ *(catch)* rats. The warden ⁸............................ *(take)* his shirt and ⁹............................ *(give)* him a blue prison one.

On the third day of his incarceration The Thinking Machine ¹⁰............................ *(try)*, without success, ¹¹............................ *(bribe)* a guard. Later that day the guard ¹²............................ *(see)* the prisoner at the window, ¹³............................ *(try)* ¹⁴............................ *(cut)* through the iron bars with a file. They ¹⁵............................ *(search)* The Thinking Machine and ¹⁶............................ *(find)* two pieces of steel in his trousers.

At four o'clock the next morning a terrible scream, ¹⁷............................ *(come)* from a cell near the centre of the building, ¹⁸............................ *(resound)* through the prison. The warden and three of his men ¹⁹............................ *(run)* to Cell 13, but The Thinking Machine ²⁰............................ *(sleep)* in his bed. Then they ²¹............................ *(hear)* the scream again – it ²²............................ *(come)* from above. Upstairs they ²³............................ *(find)* the man in Cell 43 ²⁴............................ *(sit)* in the corner of his cell. The man's name ²⁵............................ *(be)* Joseph Ballard and he ²⁶............................ *(be)* in prison ²⁷............................ *(accuse)* of killing a woman with acid. He **28**............................ *(be)* terrified because he **29**............................ *(keep)* **30**............................ *(hear)* a strange voice that **31**............................ *(come)* from far away like a ghost.

On the fourth day of incarceration The Thinking Machine **32**............................ *(throw)* to the guard outside another piece of linen with the message "only three days more". The warden **33**............................ *(can)* understand where he **34**............................ *(get)* the linen from and how he **35**............................ *(write)* the message.

At the end of the afternoon, The Thinking Machine **36**............................ *(give)* a five-dollar bill to the guard in the yard, who **37**............................ *(take)* it to the warden. But the prisoner **38**............................ *(have)* only one five-dollar bill when he **39**............................ *(go)* into the cell and there **40**............................ *(be)* a five-dollar bill with the first message!

That night they **41**............................ *(search)* The Thinking Machine's cell, and **42**............................ *(find)* nothing except for a dead rat in a hole in the floor, and five one-dollar bills in the prisoner's trousers.

About an hour later the warden **43**............................ *(hear)* the scream again **44**............................ *(come)* from Cell 43, and Ballard, who **45**............................ *(be)* terrified, **46**............................ *(confess)* to murdering the woman with acid. The warden **47**............................ *(be)* very confused.

Before you read

 1 **Listen Carefully!**

Read the text below and then listen to the first part of Chapter Five and spot the differences. There are 14 differences. Underline them and correct them.

On the fourth day of The Thinking Machine's incarceration, the warden looked exhausted. He wanted this thing to finish. He wanted his confusion to stop. But that morning The Thinking Machine threw another piece of cloth to the guard. It said "Only three days more". This time there was a gold half-dollar with it.

Now the warden was sure – he *knew* that the man in Cell 13 didn't have any half-dollars – he couldn't have any half-dollars. Just as he didn't have pen and pencil and linen. But he *did* have them. It was a fact, not a theory. And that is why the warden looked so sad.

Then there was the scream that Ballard had heard. The word acid. It didn't mean anything, of course. Ballard was obviously crazy. But there were so many things that "didn't mean anything" now that The Thinking Machine was in the cell.

CHAPTER FIVE

Countdown to Freedom

On the fifth day of The Thinking Machine's incarceration, the warden looked tired. He wanted this thing to finish. He wanted his confusion to end. But that day The Thinking Machine threw another piece of linen to the guard. It said "Only two days more". This time there was a silver half-dollar with it.

Now the warden knew – he *knew* that the man in Cell 13 didn't have any half-dollars – he *couldn't* have any half-dollars. Just as he *couldn't* have pen and ink and linen. But he *did* have them. It was a fact, not a theory. And that is why the warden looked so tired.

Then there was the voice that Ballard had heard. The word acid. It didn't mean anything, of course. Ballard was obviously mad. But there were so many things that "didn't mean anything" now that The Thinking Machine was in the prison.

END

On the sixth day, the warden received a letter from Dr Ransome. It said:

> Dear Sir,
> Mr Fielding and I will meet you in your office tomorrow evening. If Professor Van Dusen has not escaped – and we believe he has not because we have not received a letter from him – we will meet him there too.
> Yours Dr Ransome.

That day The Thinking Machine had three more messages for the warden. They were written on the same linen and referred to the meeting with Dr Ransome and Mr Fielding.

On the afternoon of the seventh day the warden passed Cell 13 and looked in. The Thinking Machine was sleeping on his bed. Everything in the cell was completely normal. "He cannot escape between now and half-past eight this evening," the warden thought.

That evening after six o'clock he saw the guard.

"Is everything all right in Cell 13?" he asked.

"Yes sir," replied the guard. "But he didn't eat much today."

The warden was feeling happy when he met Dr Ransome and Mr Fielding that evening, at seven o'clock. He wanted to show them The Thinking Machine's messages. He wanted to tell them about the events of the week. But before he could speak, the guard from the river side of the prison yard came into the office.

"The light on my side of the yard is broken," the guard said.

"Oh no. Another problem," said the warden.

The guard returned to his post in the dark. The warden called the electric light company.

"Hello. This is Chisholm Prison," he said into the phone. "One of our lights is broken. Could you send four men here to repair it? Thank you. Goodbye."

The warden went out into the yard. While Dr Ransome and Mr Fielding were waiting, the guard from the prison gate came into the office. In his hand was a letter. Dr Ransome looked at the letter.

"Incredible!" he said.

"What is it?" asked Mr Fielding.

The doctor gave him the letter. Fielding looked at it.

"It's a coincidence. 1 It must be," he said.

It was almost eight o'clock when the warden returned to his office.

"The electricians have arrived," he said. "They are working on the light now."

The warden telephoned the guard at the prison gate.

"How many electricians came in?" he asked.

"Four," was the reply.

"All right. You must be certain that only four men go out of the prison," said the warden.

---

1. **coincidence** : an occasion when similar things happen at the same time.

He put down the phone and took the letter.

"My God! It's not possible," he said, shocked.

"What is it?" asked Mr Fielding.

"It's a letter from Cell 13," said the warden. "An invitation to dinner!"

"What?" said Ransome.

The three men were silent for a long time. Finally the warden called a guard.

"Go down to Cell 13 immediately," he said, "and see if the Professor is still there."

The guard ran down the corridor. Dr Ransome and Mr Fielding examined the letter.

"It's Van Dusen's handwriting; there's no doubt about that," said Dr Ransome. "I've seen too much of it."

At that moment the telephone rang again. It was the guard at the prison gate. There were two newspaper reporters and they wanted to see the warden. The warden told the guard to let them come in.

"It's impossible," he said. "Professor Van Dusen must be in Cell 13."

Then the guard returned.

"He's still in his cell, sir," he said. "I saw him. He's sleeping."

"There. I told you," said the warden. "But if he is still in his cell how did he send the letter?"

The Problem of Cell 13

There was a knock at the door.

"It's the reporters," said the warden. "Come in."

The door opened and the two men entered.

"Good evening, gentlemen," said one. It was Hutchinson Hatch. The warden knew him well.

Then the second man came in.

"Well, I'm here," he said. It was The Thinking Machine.

The warden sat with his mouth open. He was paralysed. [1]

"How – how – how did you do it?" asked the warden, finally.

"Let's go back to the cell," said The Thinking Machine.

The men walked down the corridor to the door of Cell 13.

"Look inside," said The Thinking Machine.

The warden looked inside. Everything looked normal and there – there on the bed was the figure of The Thinking Machine. Certainly! There was his yellow hair! The warden looked again at the man beside him. "I must be mad," he thought.

Then he unlocked the cell door and The Thinking Machine went inside.

"Look here," he said.

He put his foot on the steel bars at the bottom of the cell door and three of them fell out.

"And here, too," The Thinking Machine stood on his bed and put his hand to the bars on the window. All of them came out.

"So what's this in the bed?" asked the warden.

"It's a wig," [2] The Thinking Machine replied. "Take the cover off."

---

1. **paralysed** : unable to move the body.
2. **wig** : false hair.

The Problem of Cell 13

The warden did this. Under it was a coil [1] of strong rope about ten metres long, a knife, three files, three metres of electric wire, a pair of steel pliers, [2] a hammer and a pistol. [3]

"How did you do it?" asked the warden.

"You gentlemen have an invitation to dinner with me at half-past nine," said The Thinking Machine. "Come on, or we shall be late."

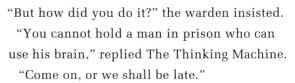

"But how did you do it?" the warden insisted.

"You cannot hold a man in prison who can use his brain," replied The Thinking Machine. "Come on, or we shall be late."

---

1. **coil** : length.
2. **pliers** :
3. **pistol** : small gun.

1 **What happened in Chapter Five? Answer the following questions.**

  a. Why did the warden look so tired on the fifth day of The Thinking Machine's incarceration?

  b. How much money did The Thinking Machine throw to the guard this time?

  c. What was the purpose of Dr Ransome's letter?

  d. Was the situation normal in Cell 13 on the seventh day?

  e. What was The Thinking Machine doing (apparently) when the guard went to check?

  f. What happened on the river side of the prison yard?

  g. Who were the two reporters who visited the prison during the warden's meeting with Dr Ransome and Mr Fielding?

  h. What was lying on the bed of the cell instead of The Thinking Machine?

Prediction

2 **We are now approaching the solution of the mystery.**

  "You cannot hold a man in prison who can use his brain."

  These are the things the warden found under the cover of his bed. What might each be used for? Did The Thinking Machine use them?

  a. a coil of strong rope about ten metres long

  b. a knife

  c. three files

  d. three metres of electric wire

  e. a pair of steel pliers

  f. a hammer

  g. a pistol

Tense revision

3 Fill in the gaps with suitable verbs in the right tense.

a. When the warden .... Dr Ransome and Mr Fielding, The Thinking Machine .... already ....

b. When the warden .... about the light, he .... feeling worried again.

c. While the three men ...., the telephone .... again.

d. The warden .... weary because of all the things The Thinking Machine .... in those days and he wished he .... involved in that bet.

e. Hutchinson Hatch .... by the warden very well.

f. The three gentlemen didn't go home because they .... for dinner where they .... the whole story.

Linking words

4 Write a short summary of Chapter Five using the following linking words or phrases.

> as a result / above all / before / especially /
> although / this is why / on the contrary /
> suddenly / if / at last

Dr Ransome's Thoughts

5 Dr Ransome was disappointed and excited at the same time about The Thinking Machine's escape. Before going to dinner he had a lot of questions on his mind he wanted to ask and he looked forward to hearing the whole story.

Imagine five questions that passed through his mind.

Before you read

 1 **Listen to the first part of Chapter Six and circle the words you hear. The words are all synonyms.**

When dinner was (*1finished/over/terminated*) The Thinking Machine turned to Dr Ransome.

"Well, do you believe me now?" he (*2enquired/asked/demanded*).

"Yes I do," (*3answered/responded/replied*) Dr Ransome.

There was a long silence. Like all the other guests, Ransome was waiting for the explanation.

"So, tell us how you did it," (*4asked/said/commented*) Fielding, finally.

The Thinking Machine (*5began/started/commenced*) the story.

"The (*6agreement/arrangement/accord*) was to go into a cell in Chisholm Prison with nothing but the necessary clothes and to (*7escape from/break out from/leave*) that cell within seven days. I didn't know Chisholm Prison. When I went into the cell I asked for three things: toothpaste, two ten-dollar bills and one five-dollar bill and to have my shoes (*8cleaned/polished/blacked*). You agreed to these things.

"I knew that there was nothing useful in the cell, so I had to use these three (*9innocent/innocuous/inoffensive*) things to help me escape. But anything is dangerous in the hands of a (*10fellow/man/chap*) like me.

"The first night I did two things. I slept and I (*11chased/hunted/ran after*) rats. You gentlemen (*12were under the impression/ thought/believed*) I wanted time to (*13organize/plan/arrange*) an escape with assistance from outside the prison. But this was not true. I knew I could communicate with anyone I wanted to at any time."

The warden (*14looked at/regarded/stared at*) him for a moment.

CHAPTER SIX

How Did He Do It?

When dinner was finished The Thinking Machine turned to Dr Ransome.

"Well, do you believe me now?" he asked.

"Yes I do," replied Dr Ransome.

There was a long silence. Like all the other guests, Ransome was waiting for the explanation.

"So, tell us how you did it," said Fielding, finally.

The Thinking Machine began the story.

"The agreement was to go into a cell in Chisholm Prison with nothing but the necessary clothes and to leave that cell within seven days. I didn't know Chisholm Prison. When I went into the cell I asked for three things: toothpaste, two ten-dollar bills and one five-dollar bill and to have my shoes blacked. You agreed to these things.

"I knew that there was nothing useful in the cell, so I had to use these three innocent things to help me escape. But anything is dangerous in the hands of a man like me.

"The first night I did two things. I slept and I ran after rats. You gentlemen thought I wanted time to organize an escape with assistance from outside the prison. But this was not true. I knew I could communicate with anyone I wanted to at any time."

The warden looked at him for a moment. The Thinking Machine continued.

END

"The guard woke me up at six o'clock the next morning. He brought me my breakfast. He told me lunch was at twelve o'clock and dinner was at six. I knew that between these times I was alone. So after breakfast I examined the outside area from my cell window. I saw that it was impossible to get over the wall. But I knew that on the other side of the wall there was a river and also a playground. The guard confirmed it. So I knew one important thing. A person could come near the prison on that side without attracting the attention of the guards.

"But there was something even more important. I saw a wire which went to the light on the prison roof. It was very near my cell window. I knew then that if it was necessary I could cut off that light.

"Then I thought about escaping through the prison building. I remembered the way to my cell. I knew that was the only way out. There were seven doors between my cell and the outside. It was too difficult."

The Thinking Machine stopped for a moment. Dr Ransome lit a new cigar. For several minutes there was silence. Then The Thinking Machine continued.

The Problem of Cell 13

"When I was thinking about these things a rat ran across my foot. It gave me a new idea. I saw there were at least six rats in the cell. But they didn't come from under the door. I ran after them and they disappeared. But they didn't go out of the door. So I knew there was another way out.

"I looked for this other way and found it. It was a hole in the floor. It went to an old drainpipe. Obviously the rats came this way. But where did they come from? Drainpipes normally go

outside the prison. This one probably went to the river or near it. So the rats came from that direction.

"When the guard came with my lunch he told me two important things. One was that there was a new plumbing system in the prison. The other was that the river was only a hundred metres away. So I knew that the pipe in my cell was part of an old system. And I knew it went to the river. The other end of the pipe was outside the prison walls.

"But before I could start work, I knew I had to distract[1] the warden. I wanted him to think that I was trying to communicate with you, Dr Ransome. So I took two pieces of linen from my shirt and wrote a message on them. Do you have the message, warden?"

"Yes." The warden looked at the coded message. "But what does it mean?" he asked.

"Read it from right to left, beginning with the 'T'," said The Thinking Machine. "Don't consider the division into words."

The warden read the message.

"T-h-i-s," he began, "is not the way I intend to escape." The warden smiled. "But what did you write it with?"

"This," said The Thinking Machine. He put his foot on the table. On it was the shoe that he wore in prison. But the polish was gone.

"The shoe polish, mixed with some water, was my ink," said The Thinking Machine, "and the metal end of the shoe lace[2] was a good pen."

The warden laughed. "Continue," he said.

"After the message the warden wanted to search my cell. This was good. I wanted him to search my cell very often. I thought, 'He won't find anything so he will stop and leave me alone.'

"The warden took my shirt away and gave me a prison shirt.

---

1. **distract** : make someone stop giving their attention to something.
2. **shoe lace** : string to tie your shoes.

How Did He Do It?

Without my white shirt I couldn't write any more messages. But I had another piece of the same shirt in my mouth."

"Where did it come from?" asked the warden. "I saw that there were only two pieces cut from the shirt. And I had both of them."

"You forget that shirts like mine have three layers of linen," The Thinking Machine replied. "I took out the inside one. You didn't notice it.

"Now that the warden was busy, I started to work on my real escape plan. I knew that the pipe from my cell went to the playground outside the prison. It is a place where boys play baseball. I knew many of the boys there. I knew that the rats came into my cell from out there. Perhaps it was possible for me to communicate with someone outside. I could use the rats.

"The first thing I needed was a long thread. [1] So I used the thread from my socks." He pulled up his trouser-legs. The strong thread at the top of his long socks was not there.

"Then on one half of my last piece of linen I wrote a message for Hutchinson Hatch. He is a friend and often helps me. I knew he would help me this time. It was a great story for his newspaper. I tied a ten-dollar bill to the letter to attract attention.

---

1. **thread** : long, very thin piece of cotton.

People always find money. I wrote on the linen: 'If you find this message give it to Hutchinson Hatch. He will give you another ten dollars for the information.' Then I wrote instructions for Hatch.

"I had to get this note outside the prison. There were two ways but the best way was the rats. I took one of them. I tied the linen and the money to one of its legs and tied my thread to another. Then I put it in the pipe.

"From the moment the rat disappeared into that dirty pipe I was nervous. The thread could break. Anything could happen. I waited. I was holding the thread and I saw that it became gradually shorter. Finally there was only about one metre of thread in my hand. I knew that the rat was outside the prison. But would Hatch receive the message?

"I had to wait. I decided to try some other manoeuvres. [1] This was to confuse the warden more. I tried to bribe the guard. I tried to cut through the bars on my cell window. The warden became very angry. He took the bars in his hands to see if they were solid. They were – then.

"That night I didn't sleep. The thread was tied to my hand. I waited for the signal from outside. I thought, 'If Hatch has received the message, and if he finds the drainpipe, he will pull the thread.' At half-past three in the morning I felt something pull the thread."

---

1. **manoeuvres** : cleverly planned actions.

How Did He Do It?

The Thinking Machine turned to Hutchinson Hatch.

"Now you can explain what you did," he said.

"A small boy brought the linen message to me. I gave the boy another ten dollars. I got some string and then some wire. I went with the boy to the playground. I looked for the end of the drainpipe for an hour. Then finally I found it. It was about thirty centimetres in diameter. I took the end of the thread and pulled it three times. The Professor pulled twice to reply. Quickly I tied my string to the Professor's thread. Then I tied the wire to the string. Professor Van Dusen began to pull it all into his cell. The wire was the most important because it could not break. The thread was too weak. It could break easily. With the wire I could transport things to the cell."

"Yes," continued The Thinking Machine. "I was very happy when the wire arrived in the cell. Then we tried another experiment. I spoke to Mr Hatch through the pipe. He heard me but it was not easy for him to understand me. I wanted some nitric acid and I had to repeat the word 'acid' several times. Then I heard a scream from the cell above me.

"With the wire it was easy to transport things to my cell. And it was also easy to hide them. I could put them into the pipe. You, Mr Warden, found the pipe but you could not find the wire. Your hands are too big. My fingers are longer and thinner so it was easy for me. In addition I put a dead rat in the pipe. You pulled it out."

"I remember," said the warden.

"The rat was there to stop you investigating the pipe," said The Thinking Machine.

"That night Mr Hatch could not send me anything useful. But

he did send me change for ten dollars as a test. The next day I continued to work on my plan.

"For this it was necessary that the guard outside saw me often at my cell window. To attract his attention I threw messages to him. I stood at my cell window for hours. Sometimes I spoke to him. He told me that there were no electricians inside the prison. If there was a problem with the lights they had to call the light company.

"This was perfect for my escape plan. There was only one more thing to do before I escaped. Once again I spoke to Mr Hatch through the pipe. It was the fourth night of my incarceration. Again Mr Hatch could not understand me. Again I repeated the word 'acid' three times. It was this that made the prisoner above me confess to murder. The guard told me the next day. The prisoner heard strange voices through the pipe. He thought it was a ghost.

"With nitric acid it was very easy to cut the bars of the window. But it was a long process. The outside guard saw me standing at my window. He didn't know what I was doing. As he watched me I cut the bars with a piece of wire covered with acid. On the night of my escape I used the same acid to cut the electric wire that went to the lights. The yard outside my window was completely dark. It was easy to escape.

"I also had a wig from Mr Hatch. It was the same colour as my hair. Yellow. I put it in the bed with some other things that Hatch sent me. When the guard passed the door he thought I was sleeping."

"But how did you get outside the prison gate," asked the warden.

"It was simple," The Thinking Machine replied. "As I said, I cut the wire to the lights before the guards turned on the current. When they turned on the current, the light on my side of the yard didn't work. The outside guard went to your office to tell you, and I escaped through my cell window. I stayed in the shadows until the four electricians arrived. Mr Hatch was one of them.

"When I saw him he gave me some workman's clothes to put on. You, Mr Warden, were standing only three metres away. Then Mr Hatch called me – as a workman – and together we went out of the gate to get something from the van. The guard at the gate knew that there were four workers in the yard. He saw that we were workers so he let us go out of the prison. Then we changed clothes and came back in. We went to your office and asked to see you. That's all."

"And the letter of invitation?" asked Ransome.

"I wrote it in my cell with Mr Hatch's pen," said The Thinking Machine. "Then I sent it through the pipe and Mr Hatch posted it."

There was silence for several minutes. Dr Ransome was the first to speak.

"Incredible!" he said. "Absolutely brilliant!"

But Mr Fielding had two more questions.

"And what was the toothpaste for?" he asked.

"For brushing my teeth."

"Why did Mr Hatch come with the electricians?"

"His father is the manager of the company," said The Thinking Machine.

"But what if there was no Mr Hatch outside to help you?"

"Every prisoner has at least one friend who will help him if he can."

"What if there was no old drainpipe in your cell," asked the warden.

"There were another two ways to escape," said The Thinking Machine.

Ten minutes later the telephone rang. It was for the warden.

"Is the light working now?" asked the warden through the phone. "Good. The wire was cut beside Cell 13? Yes I know. What's that? There are too many electricians. Two went out of the prison and there are three still inside. But only four men came from the light company."

The warden turned to the others, confused.

"The guard says that he saw four electricians come into the prison. Two went out again. But there are still three men inside," he said.

"Don't you remember? I was the extra man," said The Thinking Machine.

"Oh," said the warden. "I see." He turned back to the phone. "You can let the fifth man go. He's all right."

1 Are the following statements true (T) or false (F)? Correct the false ones.

	T	F
a. The Thinking Machine didn't tell the others how he had escaped.	☐	☐
b. He didn't know Chisolm Prison.	☐	☐
c. He had only 2 innocent things to help him escape.	☐	☐
d. The first night he slept and ran after rats.	☐	☐
e. The Thinking Machine calculated that there were eight doors between his cell and outside.	☐	☐
f. He asked Hutchinson Hatch for some nitric acid to kill the rats.	☐	☐
g. The Thinking Machine was allowed out of the prison because the guard thought he was an electrician.	☐	☐

The Key to the Mystery

2 These are the things that helped The Thinking Machine to escape. How did he actually use them?

> shoe polish   toothpaste   wire   drainpipe
> metal end of the shoe lace   socks   rats   clothes
> ten-dollar bill   nitric acid   wig   the workman's

Now go back to your predictions in previous chapters and check if you were right.

3 "Every prisoner has at least one friend who will help him if he can." Hutchinson Hatch was of great help to The Thinking Machine. How did he help him exactly?

The Press

4 The press are very interested in The Thinking Machine's escape. Write a short article recounting the whole story. (The development of the mystery is very complicated: try to include only the information that seems essential to you.)

Speaking – Role play

5 Work in pairs. One of you is a journalist, the other is The Thinking Machine. Act out the interview. Remember to include as many details as possible.

Summary

6 **Here is a summary of Chapters Five and Six of the story. Read it and fill in the gaps using the words from the box.**

linen	darkness	hear	bribes	communicate
pliers	rope	four	drainpipe	warden wig
ghostly	amazed	warden's	incarceration	
legs	bars	silver	reporters	dinner
broken	tools	thread	river	shoe lace
	wire	cut off	electricians	

On the fifth day of ¹......................... The Thinking Machine threw
another piece of ²......................... to the guard. On it was written
"only two days more" and there was a ³......................... half-dollar
with it. The warden felt tired and confused.

On the evening of the seventh day Dr Ransome and Mr Fielding came
to see the ⁴......................... . But at that moment a guard came and
told the warden that the light on his side of the yard was
⁵........................., so the warden called the electric light company and
asked them to send ⁶......................... men to repair it. Then a guard
from the prison gate brought a letter from Cell 13 inviting the men to
⁷.........................! But a guard checked and The Thinking Machine
was still in his cell, sleeping.

There was a knock at the door and two ⁸......................... came in. One
of them was Hutchinson Hatch, and the second man was The
Thinking Machine! The warden was ⁹......................... .

They all went to Cell 13 and The Thinking Machine showed them
how the steel bars at the bottom of the door and at the window fell
out. In the bed was a yellow ¹⁰......................... and under the covers a
coil of strong ¹¹........................., a knife, three files, three metres of

electric wire, a pair of steel 12........................., a hammer and a pistol. At dinner that night The Thinking Machine explained how he had done it: he had seen a 13......................... very near his cell window which went to the light on the prison roof, so he knew that if necessary he could 14......................... the light. Then he discovered an old drainpipe in the corner of his cell and realised that it probably went to the 15......................... – there was a way to have contact with the outside. He explained that the messages and 16......................... had been used to distract the warden. He had written the messages with the shoe polish mixed with water and using the metal end of his 17......................... as a pen.

Using some 18......................... from his socks he tied it to a rat and sent it down the drainpipe with a letter for his friend Hutchinson Hatch and a ten-dollar bill attached to one of its 19......................... . The message said that if the receiver took the letter to Hatch he would receive another ten dollars. Hatch received the letter and came to the outside of the prison and was able to 20......................... with The Thinking Machine through the drainpipe. He brought all the necessary 21......................... to help The Thinking Machine escape. The Thinking Machine tried speaking to Hatch through the 22......................... and asked for some nitric acid but Hatch couldn't 23......................... very well and so Van Dusen had to repeat the word "acid" several times. This was the 24......................... voice that Ballard had heard and had terrified him into confessing. With the nitric acid he was able to cut the 25......................... of the windows, and on the night of the escape he cut the electric wire that went to the lights. The yard was now in complete 26......................... and The Thinking Machine was able to get out through the window into the yard. Hatch, who had come in dressed as one of the 27........................., met him there, and gave him some workman's clothes. They went out of the prison got changed and came back in to the 28......................... office. The Thinking Machine had won the bet!

EXIT TEST

CONTEXT

1 **Answer the following questions.**

a. Where and when was Jacques Futrelle born?
b. Where did he work?
c. How did he die?
d. When did the *Titanic* sink?
e. How many people died on the *Titanic*?
f. Briefly describe the problem with the lifeboats.

COMPREHENSION

2 **Circle the correct answer, A, B, C or D.**

1. What was 'The Thinking Machine' supposed to wear for his experiment?
   A. shoes, short socks and trousers
   B. shoes, long socks, trousers and a shirt
   C. shoes, blue jeans and a shirt
   D. blue jeans and a pullover

2. The prison's guards were _____ .
   A. dishonest men
   B. cruel men
   C. very friendly and kind
   D. not likely to accept a bribe

3. The 'Thinking Machine' had to make his escape _____ .
   A. within one week
   B. within one month
   C. by the end of the year
   D. within twenty-four hours

4. What was inside Cell 13?
   A. a chair and a bed
   B. a table and a bed
   C. only a bed
   D. nothing at all

5. The Thinking Machine _____ .
   A. tried to cut through the cell window with a file
   B. tried to bribe the guard with $100
   C. tried to break the cell door
   D. killed all the rats in his cell

6. Prisoner Ballard murdered his girlfriend _____ .
   A. by poisoning her drinking water
   B. by throwing acid in her face
   C. with a long knife
   D. while she was sleeping

7. Who were the two newspaper reporters?
   A. Hutchinson Hatch and Mr Fielding
   B. Hutchinson Hatch and the author of the story
   C. Hutchinson Hatch and The Thinking Machine
   D. Mr Fielding and Mr Ballard

8. How did 'The Thinking Machine' communicate with his friend Hatch?
   A. through the cell window
   B. with a secret code
   C. with the electric wire
   D. through the drainpipe

9. What did 'The Thinking Machine' use to cut the bars of the cell window?
   A. nitric acid
   B. sulphuric acid
   C. a steel file
   D. an electric wire

VOCABULARY

3 **Match the following words with their meanings.**

1. tools	**a.** genius
2. feature	**b.** instruments
3. bribe	**c.** flat enclosed area of concrete or stone
4. flooded	**d.** terrible or tiring series of events
5. mastermind	**e.** false hair
6. yard	**f.** characteristic
7. wig	**g.** persuade someone to do something by offering money or services
8. ordeal	**h.** filled with water

VOCABULARY

4 **Relative Clauses**

Link the two sentences with a relative pronoun: *who* or *which*.

1. The prisoner hid the murder weapon. I found it in the forest.
2. The warden was old and tired. He wanted the experiment to finish quickly.
3. The cell had no furniture. It was cold and dark.
4. The boys played baseball in the playground. It was near the river.
5. One of his friends lives near the prison. He always sends him money.

WRITING

5 **Write a short paragraph.**

a. Briefly describe 'The Thinking Machine'.
b. What was your favourite part of the story?
c. Did you like this story? Why or why not?

The Problem of Cell 13

KEY TO
THE ACTIVITIES
AND EXIT TEST

Page 11 – exercise 1

1 strange   **2** thin   **3** pale
4 little   **5** thick   **6** blue   **7** large
8 yellow   **9** bizarre   **10** famous
11 unusual   **12** mental   **13** small
14 brilliant   **15** profound

Page 22 – exercise 1

a. Professor Augustus S.F.X. Van Dusen's appearance was as strange as his name. He was thin and pale, his eyes were blue, and always half-closed in concentration. He had an extremely large forehead and yellow hair.
b. He was originally from Germany.
c. His real passion was logic.
d. His nickname was 'The Thinking Machine' because he spent all his time in his lab thinking and inventing brilliant theories.
e. He was a thinker and a scientist.

Page 23 – exercise 2

b. T
c. T
d. F – He smoked cigars.

e. F – He was supposed to wear shoes, long socks, trousers and a shirt for his experiment.
f. F – It wasn't difficult because they were important men.
g. F – Dr Ransome was sorry at first, but later he thought that the experiment was a good thing because The Thinking Machine was too arrogant and he deserved a lesson.
h. T
i. F – The guards were not likely to accept even a great sum.
j. T
k. T

Page 24 – exercise 3

Open answers.

Page 25 – exercise 4

Possible answers:
a. If he had brought a gun, he could have killed the guards.
b. If he had brought a saw, he could have sawn through the bars.
c. If he had brought a notebook, he could have written some messages.

d. If he had brought a tape recorder, he could have recorded the squeaks of the rats and could have scared the guards by turning the volume really loud.

e. If he had brought a rope, he could have tied up the guards.

f. If he had brought a pair of handcuffs, he could have handcuffed the guards.

Page 25 – exercise 5

a. Dr Ransome told The Thinking Machine that it was impossible.

b. He said he had heard him say things like that before.

c. The Thinking Machine said he didn't need an explosive.

d. He asked him if he was serious.

e. He asked him what he would wear.

f. He asked the warden if The Thinking Machine could bribe his guards for twenty-five dollars.

OTHER PRISON STORIES

Page 29 – exercise 1

a. The hero of *The Count of Monte Cristo* managed to escape by substituting himself with the body of another prisoner, recently deceased.

b. Balbi used a metal spike to dig a hole in the prison roof. He found it in a copy of the Bible which had been hollowed out.

c. The film *Escape from Alcatraz* is about the only man ever believed to have escaped from the famous island prison.

d. French director Robert Bresson directed *A Man Escaped*. The story is set during the Second World War.

e. The theme of escape fascinates us so much because to escape from a cell requires a great deal of imagination.

f. Being in prison is similar to writing because just as a prisoner is trapped in a cell the writer begins with an idea in his head which he must use to liberate his imagination.

Page 39 – exercise 1

a. The Thinking Machine heard the sound of a boat as well as the sound of children playing baseball.

b. The cell was on the same floor as the prison offices.

c. First of all, the wire passed near the windows of his cell, and that could be useful. Moreover, the cell was near the ground and he was alone, except for the guard who brought his food three times a day.

d. There was nothing in his cell except a bed.

e. At the bottom of the cell door there was a space of about five centimetres between the steel bar and the floor.

f. Yes, there had been some modifications made to the prison seven years before when they had installed a new plumbing system.

g. There was a children's playground.

h. He gave him a five-dollar bill wrapped in a roll of linen.

i. The guard and the warden were

surprised because there was something written on the outside of the cloth and The Thinking Machine didn't have anything to write with.

Page 39 – exercise 2

Tapescript - the differences are in bold.

Chisholm prison was a **big** building. It was **five** floors high and it stood **near an old, abandoned church**. The wall around it was **four** metres high and impossible to climb. Even if a man escaped from his cell, he could not pass over the wall. The yard around the building was **ten** metres wide on all sides. This was the distance from the prison building to the wall. During the night, **all prisoners – no matter what their crime –** used the yard to do exercises. There were always **eight** armed guards in the yard, **two** for each side of the building.

Page 40 – exercises 3-4

Open answers.

Page 41 – exercise 5

a. But The Thinking Machine wasn't discouraged by this.
b. My food is brought here by a guard three times a day.
c. The guard had been told to watch him when he ate.
d. If The Thinking Machine hadn't been disturbed by a rat, he wouldn't have found the opening.
e. The warden saw that a message had been written on the linen.
f. A new lighting system was going to be installed by the electricity company.

Page 42 – exercise 6

1 Machine   **2** invents   **3** world
4 theories   **5** bet   **6** escape
7 permission   **8** three   **9** cleans
10 condemned   **11** walls   **12** yard
13 freedom   **14** rats   **15** drainpipe
16 window   **17** message

Page 43 – exercise 1

1 warden   **2** discover   **3** prisoner
4 got   **5** linen   **6** with   **7** decided
8 escape   **9** coded   **10** returned
11 knees   **12** catching   **13** heard
14 quickly

Page 51 – exercise 1

Possible answers:

a. The warden wanted the prisoner to give him his shirt.
b. The warden became angry because he couldn't understand how The Thinking Machine had managed to write his message.
c. On the third day of his incarceration, The Thinking Machine tried to bribe the guard to let him escape.
d. The guard refused, partly because he had only been offered very little.
e. At six o'clock the guard saw the prisoner while he was trying to cut through the iron bars of the window with a file.
f. When the guard searched the prisoner he found a piece of steel.
g. At four o'clock the next morning the warden heard a terrible scream.

Page 51 – exercise 2

Open answers.

Page 52 – exercise 3

Open answers.

Page 52 – exercise 4

a. The Thinking Machine had given the warden a piece of cloth.
b. The warden had tried to interpret the message.
c. The Thinking Machine had found lots of rats.
d. The warden had taken The Thinking Machine's shirt.
e. The Thinking Machine had tried to bribe the guard.
f. The Thinking Machine had attempted to cut through the iron bars.

Page 53 – exercise 5

Open answers.

Page 54 – exercise 6

Open answers.

Page 54 – exercise 7

FUTRELLE'S DEATH ON THE *TITANIC*

Page 60 – exercise 1

a. F – His wife survived.
b. T
c. F – The *Titanic* carried 20 lifeboats.
d. T
e. F – She took less than three hours to sink.
f. F – Most passengers didn't immediately realise what was happening.
g. T
h. T

Page 61 – exercise 2

a. 1,503 passengers lost their lives on the *Titanic*.
b. The liner had nine decks.
c. The *Titanic* was considered "unsinkable" because she was designed to remain afloat with any two compartments flooded.
d. She left from Belfast.
e. The name of the ship's designer was Thomas Andrews.
f. The life boats were designed to accommodate up to seventy people.
g. Because people thought the boats would break under the stress of a full load.

Page 62 – exercise 1

d, b, a, f, c, e

1 wrong   2 white   3 crazy
4 above   5 child   6 Ballard
7 acid   8 scream   9 warden
10 prove   11 crying   12 heard
13 take

Page 70 – exercise 1

Suggested answers:
Ballard didn't love his girlfriend. He expected her to clean the house and wash up every day, while he was out having fun most of the time. The nights before the murder, Ballard had a busy schedule as usual. On Monday night he went gambling with his friends in a sleazy bar on the outskirts of town. On Tuesday he went drinking on his own, and got really drunk. On Wednesday, while he was going out, he had a fight with his girlfriend who told him she was fed up with his behaviour. Nonetheless, he went out and didn't come back home again until it was really late. On Thursday night he went clubbing with some girls and drank a lot again, while his girlfriend was at home waiting and getting more and more annoyed. Finally, on Friday night she told him she wanted to leave him and so he took a bottle of acid and threw it in her face. She died instantly, without a murmur.

Page 71 – exercise 2

a. F – He found him sleeping comfortably in his bed.
b. F – The prisoner Ballard was scared because he had heard a voice which didn't sound human.
c. T
d. F – The message was written in English.
e. F – The Thinking Machine tried to bribe the guard with a five-dollar bill.
f. T

g. F – Ballard confessed to killing the woman because he repeatedly heard a voice shouting the word "acid".

Page 71 – exercises 3-4

Open answers.

Page 72 – exercise 5

a. The prisoner Ballard, who thought he heard voices coming from the pipes, confessed to murdering the woman.
b. The warden and the guard went to the cell where they had locked The Thinking Machine.
c. The Thinking Machine gave the guard a piece of linen on which there was a message.
d. The message the guard showed to the warden said "Only three days more".
e. The Thinking Machine, who was very good at mathematics, calculated that the moon that night wouldn't have risen before nine o'clock.
f. The voice, which sounded like a ghost, scared Ballard.
g. The warden and the guard, who were really furious about what was happening, searched the Thinking Machine's cell again.

Page 72 – exercise 6

Possible answers:
a. The warden looked fed up. He had been trying to understand where The Thinking Machine had found the linen and a pen.
b. The Thinking Machine looked exhausted. He had been planning his escape.
c. Dr. Ransome and Mr Fielding

looked worried. They had been thinking about the money they would lose if they lost the bet.

d. Ballard looked frightened. He had been hearing a strange voice.

e. The guard looked puzzled. He had been trying to understand where The Thinking Machine got his banknotes from.

Page 73 – exercise 7

1 couldn't   **2** had written   **3** didn't have   **4** went   **5** to investigate   **6** found   **7** catching   **8** took   **9** gave   **10** tried   **11** to bribe   **12** saw   **13** trying   **14** to cut   **15** searched   **16** found   **17** coming   **18** resounded   **19** ran   **20** was sleeping   **21** heard   **22** came   **23** found   **24** sitting   **25** was   **26** was   **27** accused   **28** was   **29** kept   **30** hearing   **31** came   **32** threw   **33** couldn't   **34** had got   **35** had written   **36** gave   **37** took   **38** had had   **39** went   **40** was   **41** searched   **42** found   **43** heard   **44** coming   **45** was   **46** confessed   **47** was

Page 75 – exercise 1

On the fourth (fifth) day of the Thinking Machine's incarceration, the warden looked exhausted (tired). He wanted this thing to finish. He wanted his confusion to stop (end). But that morning (day) the Thinking Machine threw another piece of cloth (linen) to the guard. It said "Only three (two) days more." This time there was a gold (silver) half-dollar with it.
Now the warden was sure (knew) – he knew that the man in Cell 13 didn't have any half-dollars – he couldn't have any half-dollars. Just as he didn't (couldn't) have pen and pencil (ink) and linen.
But he did have them. It was a fact, not a theory. And that is why the warden looked so sad (tired).
Then there was the scream (voice) that Ballard had heard. The word acid. It didn't mean anything, of course. Ballard was obviously crazy (mad). But there were so many things that "didn't mean anything" now that The Thinking Machine was in the cell (the prison).

Page 83 – exercise 1

a. The warden looked so tired because he wanted the strange events to finish.

b. The Thinking Machine threw a silver half-dollar to the guard.

c. Dr. Ransome arranged to meet the warden in his office the following evening.

d. The situation in Cell 13 on the seventh day seemed normal.

e. The Thinking Machine was (apparently) sleeping when the guard went to check.

f. The light on the river side of the prison yard went out.

g. The two reporters who visited the prison during the warden's meeting with Dr. Ransome and Mr Fielding were Hutchinson Hatch and The Thinking Machine.

h. There was a wig lying on the bed in the cell.

Page 83 – exercise 2

Open answers.

Page 84 – exercise 3

a. met / had already escaped
b. heard / started
c. were talking / rang
d. looked / had been doing / hadn't become
e. was known
f. had been invited / would hear

Page 84 – exercises 4-5

Open answers.

Page 85 – exercise 1

1 finished **2** asked **3** replied
4 said **5** began **6** agreement
7 leave **8** blacked **9** innocent
10 man **11** ran after **12** thought
13 organize **14** looked at

Page 97 – exercise 1

a. F – The Thinking Machine told his story.
b. T
c. F – He had only three innocent things to help him escape.
d. T
e. F – There were seven doors between his cell and outside.
f. F – He used the acid to cut the bars.
g. T

Page 97 – exercise 2

– He used the shoe polish to write the messages.
– He used the toothpaste to brush his teeth.
– He used the wire to transport things to his cell.
– He used the drainpipe to speak to Hatch.
– He used the metal end of the shoe lace as a pen.
– He extracted the thread from his socks to tie to the rat's leg.
– He used the ten-dollar bill to attract attention to the message.
– He used a rat to convey the thread out of the prison.
– He used the nitric acid to cut through the bars.
– He used the wig to make it look as if he was asleep in bed.
– He used the workman's clothes to sneak out of the prison gates unnoticed.

Page 98 – exercise 3

He helped him first of all by getting some wire which he tied to the string so that The Thinking Machine could pull it into his cell so he might have a sturdy means of conveying tools inside the prison. He then procured the nitric acid which the Professor would use to cut through the bars. After this, he sent him change for ten dollars.

Page 98 – exercises 4-5

Open answers.

Page 99 – exercise 6

1 incarceration **2** linen **3** silver
4 warden **5** broken **6** four
7 dinner **8** reporters **9** amazed
10 wig **11** rope **12** pliers
13 wire **14** cut off **15** river
16 bribes **17** shoe lace **18** thread
19 legs **20** communicate **21** tools
22 drainpipe **23** hear **24** ghostly
25 bars **26** darkness
27 electricians **28** warden's

1

a. He was born in Georgia, in 1875.
b. He worked on the editorial staff of the *Boston American* as a journalist.
c. He was a victim of the sinking of the *Titanic*.
d. April 15, 1912.
e. 1,503 people died.
f. There were not enough lifeboats for all of the passengers and the ships' officers did not want to fill them to full capacity, thinking that they would break with a full load.

2

1 B 2 D 3 A 4 C 5 A 6 B
7 C 8 D 9 A

3

1 b 2 f 3 g 4 h 5 a 6 c 7 e 8 d

4

1. The prisoner hid the murder weapon which I found in the forest.
2. The warden, who was old and tired, wanted the experiment to finish quickly.
3. The cell, which was cold and dark, had no furniture.
4. The boys played baseball in the playground which was near the river.
5. His friend, who lives near the prison, always sends him money.

5

a. Open answer.
b. Open answer.
c. Open answer.

Notes

Notes

Black Cat English Readers

Level 1

Peter Pan
Zorro!
American Folk Tales
The True Story of Pocahontas
Davy Crockett
Great Expectations *NEW!*
Rip Van Winkle and The Legend
of Sleepy Hollow *NEW!*
The Happy Prince and The Selfish
Giant *NEW!*
The American West *NEW!*
Halloween Horror *NEW!*

Level 2

Oliver Twist
King Arthur and his Knights
Oscar Wilde's Short Stories
Robin Hood
British and American
Festivities

Level 3

Alice's Adventures in Wonderland
The Jumping Frog
Hamlet
The Secret Garden
Great English Monarchs and their
Times

Level 4

The £1,000,000 Bank Note
Jane Eyre
Sherlock Holmes Investigates
Gulliver's Travels
The Strange Case of Dr Jekyll
and Mr Hyde
Classic Detective Stories
The Phantom of the Opera
Alien at School
Romeo and Juliet
Treasure Island

Level 5

A Christmas Carol
The Tragedy of Dr Faustus
Washington Square
A Midsummer Night's Dream
American Horror
Much Ado About Nothing
The Canterbury Tales
Dracula
The Last of the Mohicans
The Big Mistake and Other Stories

Level 6

Frankenstein
Pride and Prejudice
Robinson Crusoe
A Tale of Two Cities
The X-Files : Squeeze
Emma *NEW!*
The Scarlet Letter *NEW!*
Tess of the d'Urbervilles *NEW!*
The Murders in the Rue Morgue
and The Purloined Letter *NEW!*
The Problem of Cell 13 *NEW!*

BLACK CAT ENGLISH CLUB
Membership Application Form

BLACK CAT ENGLISH CLUB is for those who love English reading and seek for better English to share and learn with fun together.

Benefits offered:
- *Membership Card*
- *English learning activities*
- *Book discount coupon*
- *Black Cat English Reward Scheme*
- *English learning e-forum*
- *Surprise gift and more...*

Simply fill out the application form below and fax it back to 2565 1113 or send it back to the address at the back.

Join Now! It's FREE exclusively for readers who have purchased *Black Cat English Readers* !

(Please fill out the form with **BLOCK LETTERS**.)

The title of Black Cat English Reader/book set that you have purchased: _____

English Name: _____ (Surname) _____ (Given Name)

Chinese Name: _____

Address: [ ]

[ ]

[ ]

Tel: _____ Fax: _____

Email: _____

Sex: ❏ Male ❏ Female   (Login password for e-forum will be sent to this email address.)

Education Background: ❏ Primary 1-3 ❏ Primary 4-6 ❏ Junior Secondary Education (F1-3) ❏ Senior Secondary Education (F4-5) ❏ Matriculation ❏ College ❏ University or above

Age: ❏ 6 - 9 ❏ 10 - 12 ❏ 13 - 15 ❏ 16 - 18 ❏ 19 - 24 ❏ 25 - 34 ❏ 35 - 44 ❏ 45 - 54 ❏ 55 or above

Occupation: ❏ Student ❏ Teacher ❏ White Collar ❏ Blue Collar ❏ Professional ❏ Manager ❏ Business Owner ❏ Housewife ❏ Others (please specify: _____)

As a member, what would you like **BLACK CAT ENGLISH CLUB** to offer:

❏ Member gathering/ party ❏ English class with native teacher ❏ English competition
❏ Newsletter ❏ Online sharing ❏ Book fair
❏ Book discount ❏ Others (please specify: _____)

Other suggestions to **BLACK CAT ENGLISH CLUB**: _____

_____

Please sign here: _____ (Date: _____)

Visit us at Quality English Learning Online http://publish.commercialpress.com.hk/qel

BLACK CAT ENGLISH CLUB
The Commercial Press (Hong Kong) Ltd.
9/F, Eastern Central Plaza,
3 Yiu Hing Road, Shau Kei Wan,
Hong Kong